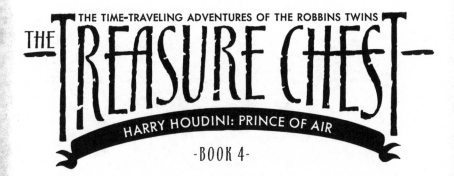

THE TIME-TRAVELING ADVENTURES OF THE ROBBINS TWINS

THE TREASURE CHEST

HARRY HOUDINI: PRINCE OF AIR

-BOOK 4-

BY *NEW YORK TIMES* BEST-SELLING AUTHOR

ANN HOOD

J
H00

Grosset & Dunlap
An Imprint of Penguin Group (USA) Inc.

GROSSET & DUNLAP
Published by the Penguin Group
Penguin Group (USA) Inc., 375 Hudson Street, New York, New York 10014, USA
Penguin Group (Canada), 90 Eglinton Avenue East, Suite 700, Toronto, Ontario M4P 2Y3, Canada
(a division of Pearson Penguin Canada Inc.)
Penguin Books Ltd, 80 Strand, London WC2R 0RL, England
Penguin Ireland, 25 St Stephen's Green, Dublin 2, Ireland
(a division of Penguin Books Ltd)
Penguin Group (Australia), 707 Collins Street, Melbourne, Victoria 3008, Australia
(a division of Pearson Australia Group Pty Ltd)
Penguin Books India Pvt Ltd, 11 Community Centre, Panchsheel Park, New Delhi—110 017, India
Penguin Group (NZ), 67 Apollo Drive, Rosedale, Auckland 0632, New Zealand
(a division of Pearson New Zealand Ltd)
Penguin Books (South Africa), Rosebank Office Park, 181 Jan Smuts Avenue, Parktown North 2193, South Africa
Penguin China, B7 Jiaming Center, 27 East Third Ring Road North, Chaoyang District, Beijing 100020, China

Penguin Books Ltd, Registered Offices: 80 Strand, London WC2R 0RL, England

Text © 2012, 2013 by Ann Hood. Art © 2013 by Denis Zilber. Published by Grosset & Dunlap,
a division of Penguin Young Readers Group, 345 Hudson Street, New York, New York 10014. GROSSET & DUNLAP
is a trademark of Penguin Group (USA) Inc. Printed in the U.S.A.

Library of Congress Control Number: 2011046306

Design by Giuseppe Castellano.
Map illustration by Giuseppe Castellano and © 2013 by Penguin Group (USA) Inc.

ISBN 978-0-448-45470-2 (pbk)   10 9 8 7 6 5 4 3 2 1
ISBN 978-0-448-45474-0 (hc)   10 9 8 7 6 5 4 3 2 1

ALWAYS LEARNING   **PEARSON**

For Gloria-Jean, who believes in magic

CHAPTER 1

Thorne Takes Charge

Maisie Robbins opened her eyes, and like she had every morning for the past three months, blinked several times to be sure she wasn't dreaming. No, she thought on this gray first day of spring, she was really awake. And she was really in the Princess Room, named by her great-great-grandfather Phinneas Pickworth in honor of Princess Annabelle of Nanuh, who had been a guest at Elm Medona one long ago summer. Nanuh wasn't even a country anymore. It had been absorbed by India in some war that Maisie had never heard of.

But the room remained, with the four-poster bed where Maisie slept every night, each post carved out of mahogany into the shapes of different animals:

giraffe, zebra, elephant, and jaguar. The canopy that stretched across the top was made of handmade, saffron-colored silk. A mural painted by the famous nineteenth-century muralist Leopold Gregg depicted a vibrant jungle scene. Sometimes Maisie thought she might actually be able to grab one of the vines painted there and swing across the room or pluck a coffee bean or mango from one of the trees.

Maisie stretched, tugging the deep green blankets tighter around her. Ever since Great-Uncle Thorne had arrived on Christmas Eve, Maisie's and her twin brother Felix's lives had been turned upside down. Great-Uncle Thorne had moved them and their mother out of the servants' quarters on the third floor where they had been living and into the mansion. He put his twin sister, Great-Aunt Maisie, back into her old bedroom, and he'd settled into his own. "The Pickworths," he'd announced on Christmas morning, "belong in Elm Medona." The local preservation society had not been very pleased with all the changes Great-Uncle Thorne had brought on, but they had no choice other than to allow the family to take up residence in the house. As a conciliatory gesture, Great-Uncle Thorne agreed to let them give tours of the mansion on the last Saturday of every month.

A timid knock came on the bedroom door.

"Hello, miss?" a small voice called.

Maisie sat up in bed. "Excuse me?" she said. "This is . . . uh . . . my room." It still felt weird to call the Princess Room hers.

"Yes, miss," the voice answered. "I'm Aiofe. Your personal maid."

"My *what*?" Maisie said.

"Miss? May I enter?"

Maisie blinked again. Several times. She must be dreaming. Not only was she ensconced in the Princess Room, but now she had a maid?

The door creaked open, and a girl who looked only a few years older than Maisie came in carrying a large silver tray. The girl had dark hair tucked under a puffy, white bonnet with a black ribbon around the edge, a full, round face with pale skin and bright blue eyes, and she wore an honest-to-goodness real maid's uniform, black with a white apron. On the tray sat a bud vase with a white rose, a silver teapot, and something steaming beneath a silver cover. All of this was on Pickworth linen, a white cloth with interlocking blue *Ps* embroidered onto it.

Aiofe put the silver tray down on the bedside table with a soft thud and big sigh.

"Heavy," she muttered.

Then, as if remembering her duties, she stood taller and smoothed her apron.

"Breakfast," she announced, lifting the silver lid to reveal two perfectly poached eggs, just the way Maisie liked them, sitting on white bread toasted to the exact color of beige that Maisie preferred; two red ripe strawberries nestled beside that; and everything on Pickworth china.

"Wow," Maisie managed to say.

"Is it all right?" Aiofe said nervously.

"All right? It's absolutely perfect," Maisie said.

Relief washed over Aiofe's face.

Maisie and Aiofe looked at each other, neither of them sure what to do next.

"Oh," Aiofe said finally, remembering.

She lifted the silver teapot and poured rich, thick hot chocolate into the cup.

Maisie stared at the cup of hot chocolate and the eggs and the toast and the strawberries.

"Um," Aiofe said, *"bon appétit."*

Then she actually curtsied. The curtsy was

followed by a blush that spread from her neck straight up both cheeks.

"Just ring when you finish," she said, indicating a silver bell very much like the one Great-Aunt Maisie had used to call the nurses when she was in assisted living.

Maisie picked up the bell and gave it a gentle shake.

Aiofe was scurrying toward the door.

"Wait!" Maisie called.

The girl stopped and turned to face Maisie.

"Miss?"

"Who are you? And where did you come from?"

Aiofe hesitated.

"Sit down and tell me," Maisie said.

She pointed to her favorite thing in the Princess Room, a seat that Maisie called the pouf. It was bright pink and tufted, a round footstool kind-of-thing that really did seem made for a princess. Aiofe sat on it almost primly and folded her hands.

"So?" Maisie said, finally digging into her eggs. The yolk ran exactly how she liked it to, giving the perfect ratio of yolk, egg white, and toast.

"My great-great-great," Aiofe began, counting

off the greats on her fingers, "great-grandmother Roisin O'Malley was the head maid for your great-great—"

"Phinneas Pickworth," Maisie interrupted.

"Yes," Aiofe said. "And our family served the Pickworths for generations until your great-aunt Maisie suffered her stroke last year."

"You mean even when she moved out of Elm Medona and upstairs, she had servants?"

Aiofe nodded. "A reduced staff," she said.

"And now *we* have servants?"

Aiofe grimaced. "We prefer the word *staff*, miss."

"Oh. Sorry."

"Your great-uncle Thorne contacted my mother and brought us all back to work here."

Maisie chewed on a strawberry. "All?" she asked.

"Well, my mother will run the household. Her sister, my aunt Emma, will be your mother's personal maid, and my sister Aine will be your brother's personal maid," Aiofe explained.

Maisie tried to keep all the names straight. Four maids!

"And of course my aunt Sarah and aunt Megan will be with Mr. and Miss Pickworth."

"Of course," Maisie said, shaking her head at this latest turn of events. What would Great-Uncle Thorne do next?

"Miss?" Aiofe said. "If you don't mind, Mr. Pickworth has called a staff meeting, and I can't be late. The butlers and chauffeurs are all assembling."

"The butlers?"

Aiofe got up from the pouf and once again smoothed her apron.

"May I—"

"Sure," Maisie said.

She watched as Aiofe hurried out. Once she'd closed the door firmly behind her, Maisie said out loud, "I have my very own maid."

Then she laughed.

She wished she had a friend she could call and tell the news. But even after six months at Anne Hutchinson Elementary School, Maisie had not acquired a single friend. Felix, on the other hand, practically had a girlfriend, Lily Goldberg. And he had a best friend, Jim Duncan. And he had about a million other friends who he was always hanging out with. Some afternoons Maisie would come downstairs and find half a dozen kids playing pool in the Billiard Room with Felix. Their faces looked vaguely familiar from school, but she didn't know any of their names except for Jim's. And she didn't like Jim Duncan, with his short blond hair and turned-up nose. In fact, Jim Duncan was maybe her least favorite person in all of Newport.

Thinking about her lack of friends almost ruined her good mood. Almost. But Maisie reminded herself that even though her parents had gotten divorced and her father had moved halfway around the world to Qatar and her mother had yanked her out of New York City where she'd lived her entire life and forced her to live in crummy Newport, Rhode Island—despite all of that—she was now out of that upstairs apartment in the servants' quarters and living in a real mansion, sleeping in a bed made for a real princess, with her very own maid.

Maisie sighed and ate her last bite of toast with the right amount of yolk and white on it. Of course, she thought as she savored the taste combination in her mouth, high on her list of good things that had happened since they'd moved here was The Treasure Chest. She and Felix had not visited that room since Great-Aunt Maisie and Great-Uncle Thorne moved themselves and Maisie's family into Elm Medona. But Maisie knew the room was right down the hall, hidden behind that wall, up the secret staircase. Already, she and Felix had gone there, touched a scroll of paper, a silver coin, and last time a jade box, and time traveled. They'd met Clara Barton, Alexander Hamilton, and Pearl Buck. Who knew whom they might meet next?

From outside came the sound of noisy car engines approaching. Maisie got out of bed and ran over to the window, parting the long, sheer curtains to peer down. She watched as a line of antique cars pulled up, one after the other. Each one looked as if it had just been polished, gleaming under the dim sun trying to peek through the layer of gray clouds. As if on cue, the driver's door of each car—twelve! Maisie counted—opened, and from each car emerged a chauffeur dressed in a dark blue uniform, complete with a stiff-brimmed hat. The men stood erect beside their cars as if waiting for something.

Maisie waited, too, holding her breath.

Just then, the sun did indeed break through the clouds, spilling bright light onto the scene below her. Into the sunlight strode Great-Uncle Thorne, waving one of his ornate walking sticks, its gold tip shining as the sunlight bounced off it.

Great-Uncle Thorne wore high-waisted, gray-and-white-striped pants; a white, high-collared shirt; and a red vest. His full head of white hair seemed extra wild, his face extra animated as he surveyed each car and each driver. When he finished, he lifted his walking stick high in the air. In unison the chauffeurs got back into the cars, and like a long snake, the cars drove around the circle of the driveway and off toward the garages where they had sat, neglected, for decades.

The large grandfather clock in the hallway outside Maisie's room chimed nine times. Great-Uncle Thorne had flown a clock maker in from Zurich, Switzerland, to get that clock back into working condition. It had taken him almost three weeks, but he'd fixed it. Every hour on the hour, chimes counted out the time, and a door opened at the top of the clock. From the door emerged a character from one of Hans Christian Andersen's fairy tales, a rotating roster of stories getting told every twelve hours. All one hundred and sixty-eight of them were represented in the clock. At noon and midnight, all the characters from one fairy tale made a final circle around the clock before disappearing inside and a new story began. Across the face of the clock, the words ONCE UPON A TIME were written in fancy script.

Nine o'clock and already the day had been full of surprises.

Maisie's bedroom door burst open, and there stood her brother, Felix, his cowlick sticking up straight, his glasses perched on the tip of his nose, and his face red with anger.

"What in the world was he thinking?" Felix practically shouted.

He marched inside, his hands gesturing madly as if his anger had taken hold of them.

"A *maid*?" Felix sputtered. "We each have a *maid*?"

"Isn't it great?" Maisie said. "My eggs were cooked perfectly. The yolks were just right and the toast—"

"Maisie!" Felix said, his eyes widening. "People shouldn't have servants. Do you know they're only nineteen years old? They should be in college or something, not working for two twelve-year-olds. This is awful."

"It is?" Maisie said. She didn't think it was awful

at all. In fact, she liked the idea of ringing that little silver bell and having someone come running.

"Of course it is," Felix said. "We're twelve years old," he said again as if she didn't remember how old they were. As if he hadn't just said it two seconds ago.

"I like mine," Maisie said. She plopped down on the pouf. "I'm keeping her."

"You sound like she's a new pet. She's a girl, you know. A nineteen-year-old girl."

Maisie shrugged, unsure what the big deal was.

"She should be out somewhere doing nineteen-year-old–type things, not bringing you eggs," Felix said. His hazel eyes blazed at his sister.

Maisie jutted her chin in defiance. Felix was not going to ruin her good day. She wouldn't let him.

"Why don't you go and play with Jim Duncan? The two of you can solve all the world's injustices."

She got up and went over to her breakfast tray.

"Meanwhile, I'm going to call my maid."

Maisie picked up the silver bell and rang it hard and long.

Almost immediately, they heard footsteps moving down the hallway.

"You're as bad as Great-Aunt Maisie," Felix said.

Maisie froze, the bell still in her hand. Great-Aunt Maisie was demanding, impossible, a complete snob. How could Felix compare her to someone like that?

"I am not," Maisie said.

"Look at you," he said. "Ringing a stupid bell for some girl to come and clean up after you."

"But it's her job," Maisie said.

Felix folded his arms across his new red Anne Hutchinson Elementary School baseball team T-shirt. That shirt bugged Maisie, too. She and Felix had both tried out for the team, and he'd made the *A* team while she'd been put on the *C* team. *You can keep your stupid* C *team*, she'd said to the coach, resigning before they even had their first practice, which, now that she thought of it, was today.

"I give up," Felix said.

He started to walk toward the door.

"Where are you going?" Maisie asked him.

"Baseball practice," he said.

Felix paused in the doorway.

"Why don't you come?" he said. "I bet the coach would take you back."

"On the *C* team? Forget it," Maisie said, angry

that Felix would think she'd consider such a humiliation.

"Come on," he said, giving her that look he gave when he wanted her to forgive him.

"No."

"Please?" he said, the corners of his mouth turning up into a small smile.

Aiofe arrived, not making eye contact with either of them, just picking up the heavy tray and rushing back out with it. All of a sudden, watching her made Maisie uncomfortable. Sometimes having Felix for a brother drove her absolutely mad.

CHAPTER 2

Abracadabra!

Felix flopped onto his bed even though he was still sweaty and his uniform was streaked with dirt. If his mother saw him, she would worry about the fine linens, the antiques, the rug hand woven in cashmere. Living in Elm Medona exhausted him. It was like living in a museum, only worse because his mother, Great-Aunt Maisie, and Great-Uncle Thorne were everywhere, watching him and breathing down his neck. If Felix could have one wish, it would be to move back upstairs to the servants' quarters. At least he could arrange his room there however he wanted, get into bed without taking a bath first, and touch anything he wanted, any time he wanted.

Samuel Dormitorio, his bedroom in Elm

Medona, especially exhausted him. Named for Samuel Santiago, a Spanish duke and childhood friend of Great-Uncle Thorne's, the room had swords and old guns hanging everywhere, a terrifying bull's head with giant horns on it staring at him from the wall directly across from the bed, and an oil painting by some famous artist of Saint Sebastian with his body pierced by a million swords above the headboard. Anywhere that Felix looked, he saw weapons or something dead.

The creepy clock beside the bed, an ornate gold thing with miniature swords for hands, reminded Felix that he had exactly one hour before dinner. He missed his mother's spaghetti carbonara. Or even good old mac and cheese. Now they had to eat in the Dining Room, where the chairs were so heavy it took two people to move one, and Felix spent all his time worrying that he might break a piece of the stupid Pickworth china. Cook, as they called the woman who made all the food downstairs in the giant Kitchen, came from France, and dinner had names that Felix couldn't pronounce. A ham sandwich with white sauce on it was a *croque-monsieur*. A big stew with every disgusting thing

Felix could imagine in it all at once was called *cassoulet*. Even worse, he had to dress up just to eat in there. Great-Uncle Thorne had dug up a tuxedo that almost fit Felix. The jacket sleeves and pant legs were too long, but a seamstress arrived one morning with a mouthful of pins and managed to hem everything by dinner that night.

Why would people want to live like this? Felix thought, not for the first time. He worried that Maisie actually liked all this nonsense.

Last night she'd shown up at dinner wearing an old dress of Great-Aunt Maisie's, a ridiculous gold thing with a matching headband that had a big feather sticking out from it and a strand of pearls that hung all the way to her knees.

"Look!" Maisie had said happily, "I'm a flapper!"

"Whatever," Felix had mumbled, yanking miserably on his bow tie.

His mother explained it away by reminding him how old Great-Aunt Maisie and Great-Uncle Thorne were.

"Who knows how long they have left, sweetie," she'd said. "It's wonderful to let them have a little bit of their old lives back."

One thing Felix knew for certain—he would *not* go back into The Treasure Chest. Felix had figured out that every time he and Maisie time traveled, Great-Aunt Maisie got healthier and younger. If they kept going back and she kept getting better, Felix would never return to his normal life as a regular twelve-year-old.

Reluctantly, he got off the bed to start to get ready for another awful dinner. Standing in the middle of the room, he glanced upward at the strangely painted ceiling. Most of the time, Felix averted his eyes to avoid scaring himself with thoughts of war and death, so he hadn't really studied the weird stuff up there. But now the giant eye painted in the very center of the ceiling caught his attention. It seemed to be looking right at him. Felix stepped back to see it better. One eye in the middle of a fist, the wrist and arm stretching across the dark ceiling.

Weird, Felix thought, shuddering.

An owl swooped from one corner, its wings opened and painted so realistically they practically fluttered. Around the edges of the ceiling, geometric symbols in black and white lined the room.

"It's magic," a voice boomed from the doorway.

Felix jumped, startled.

Great-Uncle Thorne laughed his booming laugh as he strode into the room.

"Joy of life, mercy, transformation," he said, pointing with his walking stick. Today it had a jaguar's head at the tip and the jaguar had emeralds for eyes.

"Magic symbols," Great-Uncle Thorne explained. "Clarity, truth, beauty." He paused, and his eyes grew misty. "Samuel Santiago was a magician. From the time he was a lad, he practiced magic tricks."

Suddenly energized, Great-Uncle Thorne's whole face lit up. "Why, some of his tricks are right here in this room!"

He went to the large ebony-and-ivory chest of drawers and began opening them, rifling through their contents, then slamming them shut. When he didn't find what he wanted there, he walked over to the heavy rolltop desk. With a grunt, he tried to roll the top back, but only managed to lift it a crack.

"Don't just stand there," Great-Uncle Thorne roared. "Help me open the thing."

Felix stood beside him, grabbed the edge, and on Great-Uncle Thorne's count of three, tried to lift it.

It moved another fraction of an inch, then stuck.

"This colossal abomination hasn't been opened since the Roaring Twenties, my lad. We need to put more muscle into our efforts."

Again, Great-Uncle Thorne counted to three.

Again, he and Felix tried to lift the rolltop upward.

Again, it moved a tiny bit. Then stuck.

"Damnation!" Great-Uncle Thorne shouted.

Felix cleared his throat. "What is it we're looking for again?" he asked.

"How am I supposed to know, you pudding head!"

"Um . . . pudding head?" Felix asked.

Great-Uncle Thorne raised both hands, swinging his walking stick around wildly.

"How did I end up with such idiots for relatives?" he shouted.

"If you don't mind, sir," Felix said, inching toward the door that led from Samuel Dormitorio to the bathroom, "I need to wash up before dinner."

"Fine! Go, you dolt!" Great-Uncle Thorne said.

Felix saw him put his walking stick into the gap where they'd managed to open the rolltop just before he slipped into the bathroom, relieved to be away from the wrath and exuberance of Great-Uncle Thorne.

If Felix had to pick one good thing about moving into Elm Medona, it was the bathtub as big as the entire bathroom in the servants' quarters upstairs. He needed a small step stool to climb into it. The tub was so deep that it felt more like being in a swimming pool than a bathtub. It was made of mosaics that depicted ocean life against a blue-and-green background. Starfish, crabs, an octopus, sea anemones, and all kinds of fish swam and leaped across it. Real gold glittered for scales. Real jewels twinkled as their eyes, and an oyster shell held a real pearl.

The gold faucets sent hot water, cold water, or saltwater from the ocean just beyond Elm Medona. Another set of gold spigots offered lavender, lemon, or licorice oil to scent the bathwater, and a third produced bubbles.

Felix filled the bath with hot, licorice-scented bubbles, then lowered himself into the giant bath. A compartment carved into the wall held real sponges and loofahs from the Dead Sea, and Felix chose an especially large, porous one to rub off all his baseball field dirt. Although he thought he could sit in these bubbles all night, Felix reluctantly got out so he could dress for the dinner he dreaded. *What will tonight's be?* he wondered. Fish eyes? Some kind of meat he didn't want to eat, like rabbit or venison?

Just when he slipped into the ridiculous silk robe that he'd found in the closet, in walked a triumphant Great-Uncle Thorne.

"Shuffle!" Great-Uncle Thorne ordered Felix.

He held out a deck of cards with an intricate burgundy pattern trimmed in gold leaf.

"Don't you believe in knocking?" Felix said grumpily.

"Why would I knock to enter a room in my own home?" Great-Uncle Thorne boomed. "Now shuffle!"

Felix reached his hands out. They were all pruney from the long bath.

Great-Uncle Thorne wiped them with his own silk handkerchief, then thrust the deck of cards into them.

Dutifully, Felix shuffled.

"I will now put the cards into my pocket where they cannot be touched by man or beast," Great-Uncle Thorne announced, taking the deck from Felix.

"Please observe," Great-Uncle Thorne said, "that the pocket is empty."

He leaned forward, and Felix agreed that the pocket was indeed empty.

"Now, lad, how many suits do you believe are in a deck of cards?"

Felix rolled his eyes. "I believe there are four," he said, wishing Great-Uncle Thorne would leave him alone.

"And what are those four suits?"

"Great-Uncle Thorne—"

"WHAT ARE THOSE FOUR SUITS?" he shouted.

Felix took a deep breath. "Spades. Hearts. Diamonds. And clubs."

"Clubs?"

"Yeah. You know, the little shamrock-shaped things?"

"Puppy toes!" Great-Uncle Thorne said. "Those are puppy toes!"

"Fine. Puppy toes."

Satisfied, Great-Uncle Thorne told him to choose any two of the four suits. "Announce your two choices in a nice loud voice so we can all hear you."

Felix glanced around. "All?" he said.

Great-Uncle Thorne glared at him.

"Hearts," Felix said. "And diamonds."

"Hearts and diamonds, ladies and gentlemen."

"Right," Felix said.

"Choose one," Great-Uncle Thorne continued. "Hearts or diamonds."

"Diamonds," Felix said quickly, hoping to hurry this along.

"He has chosen diamonds, ladies and gentlemen. Which leaves hearts. Every suit moves from a two all the way to a nine. I call these the low cards of the suit. Agreed? And then it moves from a ten all the way to an ace. I call these the high cards. Agreed?"

"Sure," Felix said.

"Please choose: High? Or low?"

"Low."

"Ladies and gentlemen, this young man has chosen low. Or the two, three, four, five, six, seven, eight, and nine of hearts. Of these low cards, please tell all of us which three you choose."

Felix shivered in the silk robe.

"Two, three, and four," he said.

"Two, three, and four of hearts? Wonderful. Now choose two of those."

"Two and three," Felix said, growing more and more miserable.

"Please choose one now, Felix. Of the two and three of hearts."

"The two," Felix said.

"Fantastic, dear boy! That leaves us the three of hearts. You have chosen the three of hearts! And voilà! If you remove the cards from my pocket, I believe *your* card, the three of hearts, is on the bottom of the deck."

Sighing, and certain that there was no way Great-Uncle Thorne could know this, Felix removed the deck from his pocket, turned it over, and saw . . . the three of hearts!

"How did you—"

"Aha! Now I have your attention!"

Cook made steak *frites* for dinner that night, which was just a fancy name for sliced steak with french fries. For once, Felix thought dinner tasted delicious. Maisie was dressed in the chocolate-brown skirt she'd worn for the VIP Christmas party, so she looked more like herself than last night when she'd worn that ridiculous flapper outfit. Their mother didn't have to work late for a change, and she seemed more calm and relaxed than usual because she didn't have to race back to the office.

Felix looked around the table. In the flickering candlelight, his family's faces glowed. Even Great-Aunt Maisie and Great-Uncle Thorne, seated at opposite ends and still not speaking to each other, looked younger and kinder. Best of all, Great-Uncle Thorne had shown him what he'd found in that rolltop desk: all of Samuel Santiago's magic tricks. Silk handkerchiefs, a top hat with a false bottom, a fake thumb, a magic wand, several decks of cards, and handwritten notes on dozens of tricks. Before they'd come downstairs for dinner, Great-Uncle Thorne had taught him the card trick he'd shown him in the bathroom.

"That's so easy!" Felix had said.

"Young man, all magic is easy. It requires practice, sleight of hand, and a willing audience."

Felix waited until the dinner dishes had been cleared away and everyone had finished their chocolate mousse before he stood and produced the cards Great-Uncle Thorne had given him.

"Ladies and gentlemen," Felix said, imitating

Thorne's authoritative tone of voice, "may I have your attention, please?"

"What in the world?" Great-Aunt Maisie muttered.

But Maisie beamed up at her brother, and their mother smiled at him, amused.

"Here I have an ordinary deck of cards," he began, holding it out for them to see. "Agreed?"

Maisie clapped her hands in excitement. "Oh! A card trick? I love card tricks."

Felix thought he saw Great-Aunt Maisie's eyes cloud in anger. But why would she be mad? It was only a card trick.

"Young lady," he said to Maisie, "would you be so kind as to shuffle the cards for me?"

"My pleasure," Maisie said eagerly as she took the deck. She shuffled, showing off the bridge several times.

"Thorne," Great-Aunt Maisie said in a warning tone.

Felix looked at Great-Uncle Thorne, but he was ignoring her, so Felix did, too.

"I am going to place this deck of cards in my pocket," Felix said, taking the deck from his sister.

"But first, please examine the pocket to be certain it is empty."

Great-Aunt Maisie got to her feet. She clutched the edge of the dining room table.

"Thorne!" she said again.

Nervously, Felix continued. "Empty," he said. "Agreed?"

But no one was listening. All eyes were on Great-Aunt Maisie now.

"Thorne Pickworth," she said, her eyes steely and staring across the long distance of the enormous table, straight at her brother.

"You know," she said, her voice rising with every syllable, "that there is no magic allowed in Elm Medona as long as I am here!"

"Maisie," Thorne began.

"No magic!" she shouted.

With that, she walked over to Felix and knocked the cards from his hand. They scattered everywhere— across the table and onto the floor.

Great-Aunt Maisie stormed out of the room, pausing only at the door leading out to point at Great-Uncle Thorne and shout again:

"No magic!"

CHAPTER 3

Great-Aunt Maisie and The Treasure Chest

"*Pssssst.*"

Maisie and Felix both looked up from their homework, but neither of them saw anyone. Maisie was writing sentences using this week's twenty spelling words. She liked to make up ridiculous sentences to annoy her teacher, Mrs. Witherspoon.

"Listen to this one," she said. "The *optimist eluded* the *pessimist* through positive thinking." She tapped her pen happily on her paper. "Bingo," she said. "Three words in one sentence."

"*Psssst,*" they heard again.

This time Maisie jumped up and went to peer out the door. They did their homework in the Library now, an enormous room with a vaulted ceiling with the Muses painted on it and floor-to-ceiling bookshelves that were so high ladders leaned across them to help reach the books.

Felix peeked over the top of the bloodred leather chair where he sat.

But Maisie just shrugged and sat back down in the matching chair across from him.

"Back to figuring out what x is," Felix said, chewing the tip of his pencil. He always chewed on his pencils when he did math, which he hated.

"Let's switch," Maisie said. "You write my sentences, and I'll do your math."

"Pssssst!"

From behind the enormous sofa that Phinneas Pickworth had brought back from Morocco, Great-Aunt Maisie poked out her head.

"What are you doing?" Maisie demanded.

"I don't want that cur to see me," she hissed.

Maisie grinned. "That was one of my vocabulary words last week. It's a dated insult."

"It is *not* dated," Great-Aunt Maisie said, insulted. "It's an unpleasant person, and it fits Thorne to a tee."

"Do you really need to hide from him?" Felix said.

"I'm not exactly hiding," Great-Aunt Maisie said. "I just don't want him to come with us."

Maisie and Felix looked at each other and then back at their great-great-aunt.

"Us?" Maisie said.

"I have to finish my homework," Felix said. Unlike his sister, Felix loved his teacher, Miss Landers. He would never make up ridiculous sentences or not do his homework or disappoint her in any way.

Great-Aunt Maisie disappeared behind the sofa again.

"Meet me in The Treasure Chest at nine thirty," she whispered.

The ship's clock that Phinneas Pickworth had acquired from the *SS Lorraine* read 9:15. The *SS Lorraine* had sunk off the coast of Prince Edward Island in 1892 during a hurricane, and Phinneas Pickworth had spent a fortune finding it and having it recovered—all because the ship's figurehead had been carved to look like his wife, Ariane. That figurehead stood in one corner of the Library, a wooden face made pale by years under the ocean with faded, yellow waves of hair spilling down her back. Felix thought the figurehead was creepy, but

Maisie liked it. "Who wouldn't like to be on the bow of a ship?" Maisie had said. To which Felix replied easily, "*Me.*"

"There is no way I'll find *x* in all these problems in fifteen minutes," Felix said.

"But aren't you curious about what she wants?"

Felix shook his head. "Not in the least."

"Well I am," Maisie said.

She got up and paced up and down the floor, which had a herringbone pattern called parquet.

"If I can use *predicament, exaggerate,* and *loathe* in one sentence, I'll be done," she said.

"Shhh," Felix said.

He began to read his next problem: *The sixth grade collected four more than twice the soup labels that the fifth grade collected—*

"Aha!" Maisie said, stopping right in front of Felix.

When he ignored her, she leaned her face close to his and said loudly, "Aha!"

"If *x* represents the number of soup labels," he mumbled.

"I am *loathe* to *exaggerate* my *predicament* because my brother, Felix, won't help me, anyway!" Maisie said triumphantly.

Felix sighed.

"Nine twenty-five," Maisie said. "Let's go."

"I have no idea which expression shows how many soup labels the sixth grade collected," Felix told her. "And I have five more problems after I figure that one out."

Maisie closed his math book and tugged his hand, pulling him to his feet.

"Do you think she's going to time travel?" Maisie said, her eyes bright with excitement.

"No," Felix said.

He had a pit in his stomach, the kind he got whenever his homework wasn't done and time seemed to pass too quickly. The kind he got whenever he let Maisie talk him into something he knew he shouldn't do.

"But why else would she want to go to The Treasure Chest?" Maisie asked.

Felix shrugged. "If she wanted to time travel, she wouldn't need us, would she?"

But Maisie hadn't waited for him to answer her. She was already walking out of the Library. As usual, Felix had to hurry to follow her.

Maisie and Felix walked across the Grand

Ballroom and up the Grand Staircase, past the photograph of Great-Aunt Maisie when she was their age. Great-Uncle Thorne had stuck his face in the way just as the camera clicked, so his face appeared slightly distorted in the corner. Felix always paused at that picture. Sometimes it made him feel sad to see the young girl in it and then think about how old she had grown. Sometimes it made him smile, as if he and that girl shared a secret. Tonight, though, he shook his head at that young girl. What was Great-Aunt Maisie up to?

The wall hiding the secret staircase that led up to The Treasure Chest was closed tight. Just as Felix arrived at it, Maisie pressed her hands to it, and it opened.

"Maybe she's not there," Felix said hopefully.

"Of course she's up there," Maisie said. "She just didn't want Great-Uncle Thorne to see."

Felix followed Maisie up the stairs.

Sure enough, the red velvet rope that usually hung across the door to The Treasure Chest was unhooked.

Great-Aunt Maisie stood in the very center of the room. If Maisie or Felix had expected to find her overjoyed to be back in The Treasure Chest where she had time traveled herself as a young girl, they were wrong. She looked about as angry as they'd ever seen her.

"Finally!" she said.

"We—" Maisie began, but Great-Aunt Maisie waved her hands to stop her from speaking.

"There isn't much time," she said. "Thorne might figure out where I am and show up at any minute."

"Honestly, Great-Aunt Maisie," Felix said, "no one's around. Mom is at work and—"

"Do you think I haven't planned this perfectly so that of course your mother is at work? Thorne went to a lecture on Egyptology at The Rosewood Library that goes until ten PM."

"If you knew he was at the lecture, why were you creeping around downstairs?" Maisie asked.

"Because I just confirmed for certain that he was there," Great-Aunt Maisie snapped. "I thought he said he was going there as a decoy."

"But—"

"Enough! Let's get to work," Great-Aunt Maisie said.

That was when Felix noticed that she was holding a pair of handcuffs.

"What are those for?" he blurted, imagining her handcuffing him and Maisie together and locking them up here. Maybe forever.

"What do you think they're for?" Great-Aunt Maisie said angrily. "Come here."

Maisie stepped forward.

"Not you, you nitwit," Great-Aunt Maisie said. "I need Felix."

Felix gulped. "No, no, that's all right. If Maisie would rather do it, that's fine." Even as he said it, he wondered what *it* was.

"No!" Great-Aunt Maisie bellowed. "It has to be you."

"Really, I—" Felix stammered.

"Take hold of these handcuffs this instant," Great-Aunt Maisie ordered.

Maisie gave him a little push toward their aunt. Holding his breath, Felix stepped closer, closed his eyes, and put his hand on the metal handcuffs. For a moment, it felt like the entire room held its breath.

Felix opened his eyes.

Great-Aunt Maisie stood holding the other end of the handcuffs, a look of utter disappointment on her face.

"It can't be!" she said, stomping her foot.

She glared at Felix as if he'd done something wrong.

"Are you holding on good and tight?"

Felix nodded. His heart pounded against his ribs. Was Great-Aunt Maisie trying to go back in time with him? Why? And where?

"Drat!" she shouted in frustration. "What am I missing?"

"Great-Aunt Maisie?" Maisie said. "Do you want to time travel?"

"Thorne and I used to both hold the object. It was that easy," she said, ignoring Maisie.

"Maybe if I held on, too?" Maisie said.

Great-Aunt Maisie looked at her as if she just noticed that she was in the room.

"Hmmm," she said, considering the idea.

"Maybe you need to be a kid," Felix said.

"Maybe you need a girl and a boy," Maisie said.

"Wait!" Felix said. "You need the shard! Yours is missing."

"I know that it's missing," Great-Aunt Maisie said dismissively. "I have yours."

She reached into her pocket and showed them a shard.

"You stole our shard?" Maisie said.

"I did not. Technically, it's mine. The entire house and everything in it is mine."

"Well," Maisie said. "Yours and Great-Uncle Thorne's."

"Hmph," Great-Aunt Maisie said, and turned her attention back to the handcuffs.

"No offense, Great-Aunt Maisie," Felix said nervously, "but I don't want to time travel with you. Or with anybody right now. I just want to do my math homework and go to bed."

Great-Aunt Maisie stared at him, hard.

"Actually," she said finally, "I don't really care what you want. The time has come for me to go back there, and go back there I shall."

"Where's there?" Maisie asked her.

Again Great-Aunt Maisie ignored her.

"I always assumed it took two. A girl and a boy. Your point about age can't be ignored, obviously. Thorne and I stopped when he stole the shard when we were sixteen years old. Sixteen is still so young," she added wistfully. "Isn't it?"

Maisie and Felix both knew that was the kind of question that did not require an answer. A *rhetorical* question, which was a vocabulary word from back in January.

"We all know you two can do it. But we don't know if you can take me along. If we three hold the object, and you two go without me, that won't do, will it?"

Another rhetorical question.

Great-Aunt Maisie's brow was creased with concentration.

Finally, she said, "Oh dear."

Maisie and Felix waited.

"I believe I need Thorne in order for it to work," she said.

"And Thorne refuses to do it," Great-Uncle Thorne bellowed from the doorway.

He walked in The Treasure Chest, his silk top hat still on his head and a fresh white flower in the buttonhole of his tuxedo jacket.

Great-Uncle Thorne's walking stick had a miniature solid-gold replica of Elm Medona on top of it. He held the stick by that and pointed it at each of them, from Maisie to Felix to Great-Aunt Maisie, his shaggy white eyebrows lowered above his brilliant blue eyes.

"Now," he said, "suppose you all tell me exactly what is going on here."

The walking stick was pointed at Great-Aunt Maisie.

"Starting with you, my darling sister."

"As if you didn't know, *darling* brother," Great-Aunt Maisie said. And with that, she turned and walked out.

CHAPTER 4

Locked!

Maisie sat in the corner of the Billiard Room, mentally sending bad vibrations to Jim Duncan as he set up his pool shot.

Jim practically laid across the pool table, stretching the stick and gently making his shot.

The five other kids gathered around the table all let out a big whoop. Stupid Jim Duncan had made the shot. *So much for mental telepathy*, Maisie thought.

Aiofe appeared, wheeling a cart with a pitcher of lemonade and a tray of assorted cookies for everyone.

"Whoa," Jim said when he saw Aiofe. "You've got a maid?"

"Actually," Maisie said from her perch on the

window seat, "we have, like, six maids." *Take that, Jim Duncan*, she thought.

But Jim didn't hear her. No one did. They were too busy already on to their next topic of conversation, the upcoming Talent Show at school. Jim was going to play his guitar and sing "Hotel California." Avery Mason, she of the prettiest hair in the entire sixth grade, maybe even the entire school, and Bitsy Beal, whose family was so rich she arrived at school every day in a chauffeured limousine, had choreographed an interpretive dance performance.

"You playing something on your cello?" Jim asked Lily.

"Bach," she said.

Lily had on one of her dumb vintage dresses, a paisley button-down thing that needed to be hemmed.

"Bach," Maisie said under her breath, imitating Lily.

"How about you, Maisie?" Jim asked.

Lily, Avery, Bitsy, Felix, Jim, and Daniel Dunne in his ridiculous red sailing shorts and raspberry polo shirt, all seemed to turn to look at her at once. Maisie kept her eyes on the peacock-and-peony pattern on the window-seat cushion.

The silence seemed to be about the noisiest thing Maisie had ever heard. She shifted uncomfortably on the window seat but didn't look up at Jim.

"She's going to be my assistant," Felix said finally.

"Assistant?" Bitsy said. Or maybe Avery said it. To Maisie, they were practically interchangeable.

"Sure," Felix said. "Every magician needs an assistant, right?"

"Are you going to saw her in half?" either Bitsy or Avery said.

Everyone laughed at that brilliant idea.

"Or maybe make her disappear?" the other one said.

Maisie tried hard not to cry.

Even when Felix said, "Knock it off, guys," Maisie still sat there on the window seat, the image of Pickworth peonies and peacocks blurring from holding the tears back, not moving.

"All right," their mother announced when she came home from work and into the Library, "the three of us are going to That's Amore for pizza tonight. No maids. No butlers. No Great-Aunt-Maisie and Great-Uncle-Thorne."

At the end of the day, their mother always looked so tired that everything about her seemed to droop. Her wrinkled, copper linen suit hung crookedly. Her hair fell flat around her face. And the small lines around her eyes suddenly appeared deeper and more plentiful.

"Yay!" Felix said.

He was practicing the disappearing handkerchief trick, which involved wearing a fake, hollow thumb over his real thumb, pretending to stuff the red silk into his hand while really shoving it into the fake thumb, then opening his hand and saying something like "Voilà! Vanished!" To Maisie, it looked like he was shoving that red cloth into a fake thumb. No one would fall for this trick.

"I thought Great-Aunt Maisie forbade magic tricks," their mother said. She fished a tube of lipstick out of her purse and, without looking in a mirror, slid it across her mouth, leaving a red slash.

"She doesn't know," Felix admitted.

"Just make sure she doesn't find out," their mother said wearily. Great-Aunt Maisie and Great-Uncle Thorne were wearing her out with their fighting and their various eccentricities.

Felix opened his hand, the tip of the red handkerchief poking out from the fake thumb.

"Voilà!" he said. "Vanished!"

"Hey," their mother said, impressed, "you're getting good at this magic stuff."

"I can see the handkerchief," Maisie said, pointing. "I can tell that's a fake thumb."

Felix's face fell.

"Remember what Great-Uncle Thorne said?" their mother said, shooting an angry look at Maisie. "Good magicians get better by practicing."

"How about crummy magicians?" Maisie muttered.

"Maisie!" their mother scolded.

"It's okay, Mom," Felix said. "She's had a bad day."

Maisie looked at him, surprised.

"I'm sorry Bitsy and Libby were such jerks," he added.

"I don't care," Maisie said, feeling her bottom lip start to tremble.

"Well I care," Felix said. "I told them so, too."

"I don't need you to defend me," Maisie said, even though she felt grateful to her brother. "I mean, you're my *little* brother after all."

They smiled at each other. She loved reminding him that she was seven whole minutes older than him.

"Is anyone going to fill me in here?" their mother said.

Neither Felix nor Maisie answered her.

"Okay then," their mother said, "I'm thinking Hawaiian?"

"Yuck," Felix said. "I cannot eat pineapple on a pizza."

"How about anchovies?" Maisie teased.

"How about *extra* anchovies?" their mother said, dropping an arm around each of their shoulders.

At That's Amore, after they'd eaten their pizza and the salads their mother insisted they have to counter the pizza, their mother cleared her throat in a way that made Maisie and Felix know they were either in trouble or about to hear something they did not want to hear.

"So," their mother began, "there have been some interesting changes in our lives since Christmas."

"Great-Uncle Thorne," Felix said.

"Elm Medona," Maisie added.

"And servants and fancy cars and tuxedos

and"—their mother's voice rose with each new word she said—"and . . . and . . . all sorts of nonsense!"

"I kind of like living in the mansion," Maisie admitted. "It's fun."

"My room scares me to death," Felix said. "I mean, there's a bull's head on the wall."

They started to giggle.

"How about mine?" their mother said.

They giggled even harder.

Their mother was ensconced in the Aviatrix Room. Among his many interests, Phinneas Pickworth adored female pilots. According to Great-Uncle Thorne, he'd been engaged to at least two different ones. Whenever one visited Elm Medona, he put them up in what was now called the Aviatrix Room.

"Brave Bess Coleman, Pancho Barnes, Amy Johnson," their mother said through her laughter. "And only one of them survived her flying. It's creepy living with all those dead women's pictures and goggles and leather jackets everywhere."

"But," Maisie pointed out, "you have real airplane wings hanging from your ceiling. We don't have anything that cool."

"You have tusks," Felix reminded his sister, which sent them all into a new fit of laughing.

When they had caught their breaths again, their mother took a breath.

"All of this . . . this crazy stuff going on right now, it's all temporary. You guys understand that, don't you?" she said solemnly. "Soon enough we will be back upstairs, making our own beds and washing our own dishes."

"I can't wait," Felix said.

Thinking of that apartment where they'd spent the months before Great-Uncle Thorne showed up made him miss his twin bed and the desk with the rickety leg where he did his homework and the three of them sitting around the enamel kitchen table eating spaghetti.

"I can," Maisie said. "I like being rich."

Their mother wagged a finger at her. "The problem is, you aren't rich. Great-Uncle Thorne and Great-Aunt Maisie are. I mean, even my father wasn't rich. Phinneas Pickworth made all the money and kept it in his own lineage. We grew up perfectly happy and perfectly middle class. And so will you two."

Maisie sighed dramatically. "Living inside Elm

Medona makes me feel rich," she said. "I feel special for a change," she added.

"Special and rich are two different things," their mother reminded her. "I understand, though. I do. I always felt like you do when we'd visit Elm Medona, seeing the way my father's aunt and uncle lived. Living that way for a week or so every summer. But then it was back to reality."

Maisie sighed. "I hate reality."

The waitress came over to the table with their bill, and their mother pulled out her wallet. She handed the waitress her credit card.

As soon as the girl had walked away, their mother said, "There's one other thing. I mean, it's nothing really. Or, I mean, I'm sure it won't be anything."

"Huh?" Maisie said.

Their mother blushed. "It's just that Bruce Fishbaum invited me to dinner tomorrow night. That's all."

Bruce Fishbaum was one half of Fishbaum and Fishbaum, the law firm where their mother worked about ninety hours a week.

Felix shrugged. "Okay," he said. "Don't you spend,

like, practically every minute with him, anyway?"

"Wait a minute," Maisie said, narrowing her eyes. "Are you saying he asked you out on a *date*?"

"Well," their mother said, her blush deepening. "No. I mean, yes."

"You can't go on a date!" Maisie said.

"What about Dad?" Felix asked.

"I know how awkward this must seem. It is awkward. But your father and I have been divorced for almost a year now and—"

"But what would Daddy say if he knew?" Maisie insisted. Her stomach was doing that thing it did whenever she got upset, rolling and flipping. The taste of something sour filled her mouth.

"You have to tell Bruce Fishbaum that you can't go, that you're practically married," Felix said.

"Oh dear," Maisie moaned.

Their mother fidgeted with her napkin, folding it and unfolding it, smoothing it on the table then folding it again.

"I'm sure nothing will come of it," she said.

"Then why go at all?" Felix asked.

"Oh dear," Maisie said again, standing up.

"Now sit down, sweetie," their mother said.

Maisie's hand shot to her mouth, but it was too late to stop her from throwing up all over the table and her mother's wrinkled, copper linen suit.

O—⚷

That night, as she lay in the four-poster bed with the intricately carved animals and the raw silk canopy, Maisie tried to calm her queasy stomach and her overactive mind, which was racing with terrible images of her mother and Bruce Fishbaum. Maisie and Felix had met Bruce Fishbaum a couple of times when they went to the office with their mother to pick up files or something else that had been accidentally left behind. He was tall and wiry and balding, not at all handsome like their big, burly, curly-haired father. He wore those rectangular glasses that people wore when they wanted to appear cooler than they really were, and both times Maisie had seen him, his ties had had nautical themes: tiny, fat sailboats on one, yachting flags on the other.

She couldn't stop thinking of her mother kissing Bruce Fishbaum the way she used to kiss their father, lifting her face up and standing on tiptoes to reach his lips. Worse, she pictured her actually falling in love with Bruce Fishbaum. Maybe even marrying him. Then what? Where would they live? Would they move to what he always called his "perfectly restored historical house on Spring Street," a place he liked to mention at the drop of a hat? Would they have to share rooms with his two kids, the boy and girl whose pictures on sailboats and in hockey gear grinned out from his desk? Maisie did not want to share a room with Allison Fishbaum, expert sailor and ice-hockey goalie.

All of this thinking made her feel like she might throw up again.

Groaning, Maisie got up and went into the Princess Bathroom, a Pepto-Bismol–pink confection that made her even queasier. Princess Annabelle had apparently loved this very shade of pink, and everything here—sink, bathtub, shower stall, even the toilet—shone pinkily at Maisie. The tiles on the walls were the same pink, except inlaid on each one was a jewel of some kind. If you stood in the center of the room you could play a kind of connect the dots with the jewels and see they formed a giant crown, an exact replica of Princess Annabelle of Nanuh's tiara. All that pink and sparkle forced

Maisie to get on her knees, hold her hair back in a messy ponytail, lean over the toilet, and throw up some more.

After she'd finished, she made her way on her wobbly legs back to bed. If they'd been in their apartment on Bethune Street or even upstairs in the servants' quarters, someone would have heard her being sick and come and held her hair back, given her some ginger ale, and tucked her back in. But Elm Medona was so enormous that no one heard anything going on. Maisie felt lonely and sad and miserable.

When she heard the door creak open, she expected to see her mother standing there. Instead, Great-Aunt Maisie—dressed in an old-fashioned, ivory silk dress, her hair twisted into an updo, and her Chanel Red lipstick in place—stood illuminated by the moonlight streaming in from the large hall window behind her.

"Get up," Great-Aunt Maisie ordered. "I have a plan."

"Doesn't anybody know I've been throwing up?" Maisie cried. "I could have died in here and no one would even care."

"Pshaw," Great-Aunt Maisie said. "Stop being so melodramatic and get up this instant."

"Fine," Maisie said, throwing back the covers and climbing out of bed.

Great-Aunt Maisie frowned at her. "What in the world are you wearing?" she demanded.

Maisie looked down at her plaid pajama bottoms and Mets fleece vest.

"You cannot go looking like that," Great-Aunt Maisie said, her voice dripping with distaste.

"Where are we going?" Maisie said.

"That's for me to know and you to find out."

Maisie rolled her eyes. "Honestly," she muttered.

But she dutifully went into the walk-in closet and changed from her pajamas into her jeans and an old peasant blouse she'd rescued from her mother's giveaway bag when they were moving from New York. The blouse was white and scoop-necked and flowy, with red and yellow and black flowers embroidered along the bottom. Her mother had bought it in Mexico on her honeymoon. Maisie stepped into her black flip-flops and went back to Great-Aunt Maisie.

"Satisfied?" she said.

Great-Aunt Maisie sniffed. "You look like a ragamuffin, but I guess it'll do."

She grabbed Maisie's arm and led her out into the hall.

"We have to be quiet," she whispered as they tiptoed across the hall.

At the wall that hid the stairs to The Treasure Chest, Great-Aunt Maisie paused.

"You and I are going on an adventure," she said.

Maisie smiled. Going on an adventure with Great-Aunt Maisie was the perfect way to escape her mother's date with Bruce Fishbaum, having to be Felix's assistant at Talent Night, all of it.

"Excellent," Maisie said.

Great-Aunt Maisie pressed her palm to the wall. It opened easily, and she took Maisie's hand in hers like they were best friends. They made sure the wall closed behind them. At the foot of the secret stairs, Great-Aunt Maisie reached into her white, fringed purse and pulled out the handcuffs.

Maisie gasped. "You took those from The Treasure Chest?"

Great-Aunt Maisie grinned at her. "In a way," she said. "I've had them for over eighty years."

"What?"

"I'll explain upstairs," Great-Aunt Maisie said. "There's no time for chitchat. Who knows what Thorne is up to, that dog."

Maisie followed her great-aunt up the stairs.

But at the top, Great-Aunt Maisie stopped abruptly.

"Damnation!"

"What's wrong?" Maisie asked, trying to see past her.

"What's wrong?" Great-Aunt Maisie said, stepping aside.

Maisie looked in disbelief.

The door to The Treasure Chest was closed. Heavy chains hung across it, and three padlocks gleamed from them.

"It's locked!" Maisie said.

Great-Aunt Maisie lifted her fist into the air. Her eyes seemed to be on fire and her face contorted with wrath.

"Thorne!" she said. "Irascible, impossible idiot! Thorne!"

CHAPTER 5

The Talent Show

Felix sat in Samuel Dormitorio—he found it hard to think of it as *his room* instead of Samuel's Dormitorio—practicing his magic act for the Talent Show the next night. At least he tried to practice. Somewhere downstairs his mother was waiting for Bruce Fishbaum to drive up in his BMW and take her on a date. An actual date. Felix did not . . . no, he *could* not witness any part of this.

Earlier, he'd seen his mother bustle past with shopping bags, smelling like she'd tried on every perfume they offered at the Macy's perfume counter. Her cheeks looked flushed, and her hair looked freshly styled. She'd smiled at him, but he pretended he didn't notice any of it: the shopping bags, the blown-out hair, the smile. Instead, he met her eyes with a flat, unflinching gaze that he hoped she read as: *How could you betray Dad like this? How could you betray all of us? With Bruce Fishbaum of all people?*

"I still see the red tail of the handkerchief," Maisie announced as she marched into the room.

Felix sighed. He pulled the handkerchief out of the fake thumb and started over, flapping it open with a dramatic flourish.

Maisie walked over to the window and peered out. From this room, you could see part of the driveway. The part where Bruce Fishbaum's car would appear at any minute.

"Don't look," Felix said gently. "It'll only make it worse."

"Note that he's already ten minutes late," Maisie said without turning her attention from the driveway below.

"Who?" Felix said casually.

Even though he couldn't see his sister's face, he could picture her rolling her eyes.

"Maybe he won't come," Maisie said. "Maybe he'll stand her up." Then she added under her breath, "Serves her right."

"Ladies and gentlemen," Felix said to the bull's head on the wall. "Here I have an ordinary silk handkerchief—"

"An *ordinary* silk handkerchief?" Maisie snorted.

"As you can see, I have nothing in my hands—"

Maisie spun around to face him. "How can you be practicing magic tricks at a time like this?" Her nostrils flared and her eyebrows furrowed, not unlike the bull's head.

"If I'm concentrating on this," he said, waving the handkerchief, "then I don't have to think about—"

As if on cue came the sound of a car pulling into the driveway.

Despite his determination to avoid anything about this date of their mother's, Felix ran to the window, too. He stood beside his sister and watched as Bruce Fishbaum emerged from his shiny silver BMW.

Maybe Bruce Fishbaum was once considered handsome, Maisie conceded. But now his hair was salt-and-pepper bristles cut short around a big bald head. He had on a blue-and-white-striped button-down shirt and a tie that no doubt had a nautical theme. Blue jeans. The gut hanging over the belt.

"Ugh," Maisie said. "Look at him."

Felix did, his heart doing funny flips the whole time.

"He's fat," Maisie said.

Felix watched the top of Bruce Fishbaum's head, his bald, tanned scalp, disappear. He swallowed hard.

"He's—" he began.

"Bald," Maisie finished for him.

"He's—"

"Conceited? Full of himself?"

Felix swallowed hard again.

"He struts!" Maisie said. "Like a rooster!"

His sister's face grew blurry through Felix's tears. He shook his head.

"He's not Dad," Felix finally managed to say.

"I've been thinking," Maisie said later that night as she and Felix lay in wait in the Library for their mother's return.

They had eaten two bags of microwave popcorn, the extra buttery kind; the funny-shaped lemon cookies that Cook had made earlier; the ends of three different kinds of ice cream; a sleeve of saltines and a bag of stale miniature marshmallows. And still their mother was not home.

Felix's eyes threatened to droop shut, but as soon as his lids began to close he saw an image of his mother kissing Bruce Fishbaum, like a scene in a movie, and he bolted wide awake again.

"Are you listening?" Maisie demanded.

"Yes," Felix said through a yawn.

"I've been thinking about Great-Uncle Thorne."

"Was that a car?" Felix said, getting to his feet quickly.

He waited.

Nothing.

Disappointed, he plopped back down on the red leather sofa.

"Where has he been all this time?" Maisie said.

When Felix didn't answer her, she poked him.

"Huh?" she said. "Where?"

"London?" Felix said. "I thought he said something about London."

"Yes, but *where* exactly?"

"How should I know? I don't know anything about London," Felix said, exasperated. Who cared about Great-Uncle Thorne's former address when their mother was out kissing Bruce Fishbaum?

"But was he in a house? Alone?"

"Maisie?" Felix said. "What's your point?"

"My point is that I think we brought him back, too."

"Back?" He sat upright. "Was that a car?"

Maisie sighed one of her big dramatic sighs. "I think he was old and decrepit," she paused, mentally searching her vocabulary words. "Infirmed," she continued triumphantly. "Just like Great-Aunt Maisie. And our time traveling revived him, too."

Felix twisted his face free from her grasp.

"Well," he said, "that makes sense, I guess."

Maisie looked at him expectantly.

"Don't you see?" she said, frustrated.

Felix slumped back into the sofa. "I guess I don't," he admitted.

"We're twins, right?"

Felix nodded, even though this was yet another rhetorical question.

"And so are Great-Aunt Maisie and Great-Uncle Thorne, right?"

And another one, Felix thought.

Maisie leaned closer to him. He could smell her fake butter, lemon cookie, mint chocolate chip, salty breath.

"That's the missing piece," she said. "You need to be a twin to do it."

Felix sat upright again.

"You need to be a twin to do it," he repeated slowly.

Their mother's voice cut through the room.

"You need to be a twin to do what?" she said.

O—⚷

Maisie and Felix sipped the hot chocolate their mother made for them and studied her face for signs of love.

She had taken them down to the vast Kitchen, with all its gleaming stainless steel and subway-tiled walls and industrial-sized everything after they'd jumped up and shouted: "You need to be a twin to understand!"

"Understand what?" she'd said with that tone of voice that let them know she knew they were up to something.

"To understand . . . being a twin!" Maisie had said, and Felix had nodded enthusiastically beside her.

"Hmm," their mother had said. She'd stared at them a few seconds more, then thrown her hands up in surrender. "I think we all need some hot chocolate," she'd said finally.

The hot chocolate was made with unsweetened chocolate, cream, vanilla, cinnamon, and a touch of chili pepper in it, just the way they liked it. Maisie and Felix knew that their mother had learned to make hot chocolate this way on her honeymoon in Mexico with their father. They took it as a good sign that she made it for them now, fresh off her date with Bruce Fishbaum.

She peered at them from over the rim of her mug.

"Were you two actually waiting up for me?" she said.

"Yes," Felix said at the very same time that Maisie said, "No."

"Bruce Fishbaum and I are just friends," their mother said. "FYI."

FYI? Maisie thought in horror. Their mother didn't say things like "FYI." That was definitely Fishbaum-speak.

"But he wore a tie," Felix pointed out.

Their mother laughed. "He always wears a tie. Twenty-four seven."

24-7? More Fishbaum-speak!

"But it's so late," Felix said.

"We got caught up discussing the Holbrook case," their mother said.

Felix tried to give her the same look she gave

them, the one that let her know he didn't buy what she was saying. Not for an instant.

They each sipped their hot chocolate in silence.

Then their mother said, "Twins run in the Pickworth family."

"Obviously," Maisie said.

"Even Phinneas was a twin," their mother said.

"Who was his twin?" Felix asked her.

"Amy Pickworth." She shook her head sadly. "She disappeared in the Congo or somewhere when she was only sixteen."

"And they never found her?" Felix said.

Their mother shook her head again. "Sad," she said, collecting the empty mugs.

She yawned. "Some of us have work tomorrow," she said.

"On Saturday?" Felix said, trying not to whine.

"The Holbrook case," their mother said.

Maisie narrowed her eyes. That meant Bruce Fishbaum again.

"But you're coming to the Talent Show, right?" Felix asked.

Their mother smoothed his cowlick. "Wouldn't miss it," she said.

In that moment, Felix chose to believe that his mother and Bruce Fishbaum really were just friends, colleagues, and workers on the Holbrook case. But when he met Maisie's eyes, he knew his sister didn't believe that. Not one bit.

A buzz ran through the crowd in the Anne Hutchinson Elementary School auditorium as Felix, Maisie, and their mother arrived with Great-Uncle Thorne and Great-Aunt Maisie for the talent show. Thorne and Maisie Pickworth were legendary among so many of the Newport families there. Stories about them—their eccentric father, the grand parties thrown at Elm Medona, even the rumors that Elm Medona was haunted—still swirled around at cocktail parties and fund-raisers in certain circles.

Great-Aunt Maisie cut quite a figure in her vintage navy blue Chanel suit, her back erect, her head held high, a flat-brimmed boater sitting at an angle atop her white hair. Behind her, Great-Uncle Thorne rhythmically tapped his walking stick with the replica of Elm Medona on it along the polished hardwood floor. He wore a violet three-piece suit with a lavender-and-white-striped shirt and a bow tie covered in every shade of purple polka dot imaginable.

"Fop," Great-Aunt Maisie had said to him when they got in the car.

"Prig," he'd said right back to her.

"Dandy!" she'd shouted.

"Stop, you two!" Maisie and Felix's mother had ordered them, just the way she would have ordered Maisie and Felix. "Honestly," she'd muttered.

Unlike Great-Aunt Maisie, who kept her blue eyes focused straight ahead as they moved down the central aisle of folding chairs, Great-Uncle Thorne made eye contact with just about everyone who dared make eye contact with him. His bushy white eyebrows wiggled, and his head bobbed back and forth.

Felix felt embarrassed to have everyone watching them. He was nervous enough about his magic act. Now he had to have just about the entire audience whispering about the Pickworths and wondering how old these two must possibly be and where they'd been for so many years. He glanced up at Maisie, but she had a bemused, almost happy look on her face as if she enjoyed all the attention.

Finally they reached the front row where three pieces of printer paper with RESERVED PICKWORTHS written on them in black marker sat on the three center seats.

"Reserved?" their mother asked, confused.

She walked last in their little group, following Great-Aunt Maisie's lead.

"Of course," Great-Aunt Maisie said haughtily. "The Pickworths always have their seats reserved."

"In the front row," Great-Uncle Thorne added.

That was probably the first thing those two had agreed on since he'd shown up at Christmas.

"Center," Great-Aunt Maisie said, sitting in the center seat of the three reserved ones as if to finalize her point.

"Well, it's just a school show," Felix and Maisie's mother said dismissively. "Honestly. No need to put people to so much trouble."

Great-Aunt Maisie shifted in her seat and held up the printer paper she'd sat on.

"Jennifer," she said, her voice icy, "I hardly think anyone was put out by taking some paper, scribbling on it, and tossing it on some rickety folding chairs."

She shifted again. "Chairs that feel like they were retrieved from a trash heap," she added. "Pickworths always went to the Field School."

"The Field School closed in 1969," their mother said.

"We have to get backstage," Felix said.

"Break a leg, you two," his mother said.

Great-Aunt Maisie nodded in their general direction, and Great-Uncle Thorne ignored them completely as they left the auditorium to get ready.

O—⚡

Despite her earlier reluctance, Maisie seized on her role as magician's assistant to Felix. She slipped on her black-ruffled tulle skirt, tights decorated with silver stars, and her mother's old, high black platform shoes. On top, she wore a faded leotard, but she threw a dramatic cape over her shoulders. The cape was also black, but the lining was an iridescent blue. Maisie made Felix sprinkle almost an entire tube of glitter on her.

"Don't forget the hair," she told him, scrunching her eyes shut.

"You sparkle everywhere," Felix said when he'd finished, stepping back to examine his handiwork.

He wore the tuxedo that almost fit him and Great-Uncle Thorne's top hat. From behind the curtain, Maisie and Felix watched Lily Goldberg play her cello. Felix wished he could have asked Lily to be his assistant, especially for the handcuff trick that Great-Aunt Maisie had shown him. Though she didn't want magic in the house for a reason Felix didn't understand, she seemed very interested in the handcuff trick and that he do it just right.

"Remember," she'd advised, "it is not the trick that is to be considered, but the style and manner in which it is presented."

Then Great-Aunt Maisie had explained to him that all he had to do was have his assistant give him a kiss for luck, handcuff him so that his hands were behind the chair he sat in and away from the audience, give the handcuff key to a member of the audience, then distract everyone by swirling her cape dramatically and leaping around like a crazy person.

"And I get out of these handcuffs how?" Felix said.

He had no desire to get stuck handcuffed to a chair and have to get the dumb things sawed off him.

"I'm satisfied with the disappearing handkerchief, you know," he'd said.

But Great-Aunt Maisie was practically jumping

with excitement. "Here's the thing," she said excitedly, clapping her hands together. "The key Maisie gives to someone in the audience isn't the real key."

"Okay," Felix said. "So where is the real key?" His wrists itched just thinking about this trick going badly wrong.

Great-Aunt Maisie opened her mouth and pointed.

"In my mouth?" Felix said.

"Not your mouth, you dolt. In your assistant's mouth. When she kisses you good-bye, she slips it into your mouth—"

"Gross! I'm not having a key that was in Maisie's mouth slipped into mine. By my sister? No way."

Great-Aunt Maisie shook her head, disgusted. "Of course not. You choose the most beautiful girl you know and ask her to do it."

Felix thought about Lily Goldberg and blushed. Thankfully, Great-Aunt Maisie didn't notice. She just kept on explaining.

"And while your beautiful assistant is twirling and spinning like Isadora Duncan, you—"

"Who?" Felix asked.

"Don't you know anything?" Great-Aunt Maisie

said. "Isadora Duncan is only one of the most famous dancers who ever lived. Poor thing. Such a tragic end." She sighed. "Why am I even bothering to teach you this trick?"

"Exactly," Felix told her. "I've got the card trick and the disappearing—"

"Two tricks?" she bellowed. "You call that a magic act?"

"It's just the school Talent Show," Felix mumbled.

"While she's cavorting around the stage, you take that key and unlock the handcuffs. Abracadabra! You are a handcuff escapist."

Felix pondered the trick. Lily Goldberg slipped the key into his mouth. He removed it and hid it in his hand until the handcuffs were locked. She cavorted as Great-Aunt Maisie called it, and abracadabra, he was free. And he got a chance to have Lily Goldberg's mouth on his mouth for a second or two.

Watching Lily now, he couldn't help but wonder what it would feel like to have her kiss him for luck and slip him the key.

Then he caught sight of Maisie standing in the wings waiting, glittering like crazy and chewing her bottom lip.

Lily finished.

The audience gave her a standing ovation, then the lights went dark for five seconds and Maisie and Felix took the stage.

The card trick went without a hitch.

The disappearing handkerchief, thanks to the distance from the front row to the stage, also got big applause.

Then Felix announced his final trick.

"That's right, ladies and gentlemen," he said in his best magician-sounding voice, "my assistant here will handcuff me to this chair, and I will free myself before you can count down from ten."

Maisie stood in the spotlight. She handcuffed him to the chair.

"And now, my assistant Lily Goldberg will join us."

"What?" Maisie said.

Lily Goldberg came on the stage.

"Felix?" she said. "May I give you a kiss for luck?"

"Well," he said reluctantly, "I guess so."

The audience laughed.

Felix tried not to look at his sister, whose face had filled with betrayal and disappointment.

Lily made her way to him, walking on exaggerated

tiptoes. She bent primly at the waist and slipped the key from her mouth to his. Felix thought he might faint from the brief contact her lips made on his, almost like a butterfly landing on them.

Maisie stood awkwardly onstage, feeling yet again like a third wheel. She might never talk to her brother again. From the stage, she could see her mother and Great-Aunt Maisie and Great-Uncle Thorne perfectly. Her mother beamed up at her, but the other two sat unmoving and seemingly unmoved. Even as Maisie dramatically threw the fake key into the audience and handcuffed Felix to the chair, their expressions didn't change.

"Let's start the countdown," Maisie said. "Ten . . ." Let Lily Goldberg feel like the outsider, she decided.

The audience joined in, and Maisie leaped and twirled her cape.

At three, Felix's hands shot into the air, the handcuffs swinging, unlocked.

Maisie thought she saw Great-Aunt Maisie give the smallest smile then, but she couldn't be sure. People jumped to their feet, clapping like crazy, and her family got lost in a blur of faces.

While their mother went to get the car, Felix and Maisie stood by the entrance to the stage door with Great-Aunt Maisie and Great-Uncle Thorne.

"It was great, wasn't it?" Maisie asked them.

"Entertaining," Great-Uncle Thorne said.

"Felix is actually getting good at magic tricks, isn't he?" Maisie persisted, taking off her cape.

"Oh," Great-Aunt Maisie said, "I've seen better."

Felix scowled at her.

"Here's the handcuffs you loaned me," he said.

Suddenly, Great-Uncle Thorne grew animated.

"*You* loaned him those?" he roared.

The handcuffs dangled between the four of them.

"That's right," Great-Aunt Maisie said. "They're mine."

"Don't give them back to her," Maisie said, grabbing the handcuff that Felix wasn't holding.

"Felix!" Great-Uncle Thorne said. "Put them away!"

"No!" Great-Aunt Maisie said. "You know they're mine, Thorne."

She tried to yank them free from Maisie's and Felix's grasps, but Great-Uncle-Thorne was yanking them in the other direction.

The smell of Christmas trees filled the air. And vanilla. And salt water.

Felix and Maisie felt themselves being lifted and tossed and pulled. Their eyes opened wide in disbelief. What was happening? Great-Uncle Thorne somersaulted beside them, his face bewildered. Then Great-Aunt Maisie shot past them, her mouth opened into a happy *O* of surprise and delight.

They tumbled and rolled, faster and faster.

But where were they going? And how?

There was no time for answers. Like that, Great-Aunt Maisie, Great-Uncle Thorne, Felix, and Maisie were gone.

CHAPTER 6

Coney Island

Even though Felix landed hard, his back crashing onto a wooden floor, he still oddly had the sensation of moving. Moving slowly. Upward.

He opened his eyes and saw a sea of high-button boots, long skirts, and stiff trousers.

"Little boy," a woman with a feathered hat scolded, "get back up here or you'll fly off."

Felix pulled his aching self up to a sitting position. He was facing about a dozen people sitting on a wooden bench, staring down at him.

He grinned up at them and took the hand of a man with a mustache even bigger than Great-Uncle Thorne's, letting the man help him to his feet. Everyone scrunched over so that he could squeeze in.

In the distance, Felix saw the ocean glittering bright blue. Combined with the sky, equally as blue and sprinkled with perfect white fluffy clouds, he felt as if he had landed smack in the middle of a postcard. A postcard that was definitely going up a hill along a creaky track. The people around him looked like they had stepped out of a postcard, too, with their big hats and suits and funny shoes.

A few of the women were holding hands tightly and staring all wide-eyed and scared.

"It's my first time," one of them said. She had hair in big, bouncy banana curls, and the tip of her nose was sunburned.

"Mine too," the dark-haired one beside her said in a quivering voice.

Felix nodded at them as if he understood. Shifting his gaze in the other direction, away from the ocean, he saw a giant fake elephant. There appeared to be people standing on top of it.

The car reached the top, paused, then coasted down the track.

Everyone except Felix screamed or gasped or laughed nervously.

Felix smiled. Wherever he had landed, this was a

roller coaster. The slowest roller coaster he'd ever been on.

From between the banana-curled girl and the dark-haired girl's legs, Maisie's head popped out.

"What was that?" she said, laughing.

The man with the giant mustache glared at her.

"Young lady," he said. "You have just taken a ride on the Gravity Pleasure Switchback Railroad."

"I have?" she said, scrambling to her feet.

The roller coaster had come to a stop, and everyone was getting out. But instead of leaving the ride, they were getting into another car.

The girl with the banana curls fanned herself wildly. "I thought I was going to faint," she said. "Didn't you?"

Her dark-haired friend nodded and wiped her forehead with a small white handkerchief.

Maisie and Felix tried not to laugh as they followed them out of the car and onto another one.

"Now what?" Maisie asked.

"We're switching tracks," a woman explained. "So that we can go up that hill."

Once again, the car crept up a hill along a wooden track, going slower than the speed limit on Thames

Street back in Newport. Once again, it paused at the top, then made its rickety way down. As the people around them screamed and closed their eyes, Maisie and Felix laughed.

A few summers ago, their father had taken them to Coney Island, where they'd ridden an old wooden roller coaster called The Cyclone. Felix, terrified, could only do it once. But Maisie and their father rode it over and over again, her squeals filling the salty amusement park air. Their father had told them that at the turn of the twentieth century, amusement parks were built at seaside resorts like Coney Island and Atlantic City and all along the coast of New England. Most of those parks were long gone now, he'd said. A lot of them got destroyed by fires because everything in them was made of wood. Others had closed due to neglect. Surely they were in one of them right now.

Felix studied the clothes of the people sitting on the bench with them. Yes, they looked like people from the turn of the century. And there was the ocean in the distance. He even heard the sound of the music that played on merry-go-rounds.

The car came to a halt, and everyone stood to disembark.

Maisie grabbed Felix's arm and pointed to the words written in lights across an arch.

"How did we get so lucky?" she said.

Felix read the words out loud.

"Coney Island," he said.

O—➤

To time travel and land in an amusement park—and not just any amusement park but an amusement park in New York—made Maisie about as happy as she could be. Not only could they ride rides all day (although she hoped the other rides were better than that lame roller coaster), eat hot dogs, and walk on the beach, but she could pretend she lived back here and at the end of the day get on the F train and head home. Almost a perfect day. Except for one thing: Where were Great-Aunt Maisie and Great-Uncle Thorne?

If she asked Felix, he would get all worried, and there would go their day of fun. He would want to find them, and instead of getting on . . . Maisie tried to take in everything she was seeing and decide what to do next . . . there! That Ferris wheel over there. Instead of riding that, they would have to walk up and down looking for two cranky old people.

"Look!" she said to her brother. "Let's go on the Ferris wheel."

The sign in front of it said: WORLD'S LARGEST FERRIS WHEEL. Which it wasn't. The thing had only twelve cars and moved excruciatingly slow.

Still, she grabbed Felix's arm and pulled him toward it. Her plan, she decided, was to keep him too busy to wonder about Great-Aunt Maisie and Great-Uncle Thorne. Eventually they would find whomever they needed to find, give him or her the handcuffs, then go back home. For all they knew, Great-Aunt Maisie and Great-Uncle Thorne were still standing in the auditorium at Anne Hutchinson Elementary School, fighting over the handcuffs.

Maisie stopped suddenly.

The handcuffs. Who had the handcuffs? She didn't. She lifted her hands in front of her face just to be sure. Her black, tulle magician's assistant skirt didn't have any pockets, and neither did the old leotard she had on from her misguided efforts at a ballet class last year. The thing had small pils all over it and was just tight enough to be uncomfortable and ride up her butt. No pockets there.

She glanced at Felix, who was staring at the Ferris

wheel with a worried expression. Maybe he had the handcuffs in his pocket? But if she asked him that, and he didn't have them, then he would get worried about how they were ever going to get home and their day would be ruined. Maisie sighed over all the things she had to keep quiet about so that Felix would stay calm.

"World's largest Ferris wheel!" she said, continuing toward it.

This time, Felix took her arm and stopped her.

"Wait a minute," he said. "We have to pay for a ride."

He pointed to a sign.

"Five cents, to be exact," he said.

Of course they had to pay, Maisie scolded herself. How could she be so dumb? Somehow they had to find some money. She wasn't going to be at Coney Island on a beautiful day and not ride the rides.

Maisie's face brightened.

"Uh-oh," Felix said. Clearly she'd come up with a scheme that he would no doubt not want to be part of.

"Do you have your cards with you?" she asked.

"Yes," he said carefully.

"Well then, we'll have to get to work, won't we?" Maisie told him.

Performing card tricks on the runway of Coney Island was one of the last things Felix wanted to do. But he recognized the determination in his sister's eyes. No matter what he said, he would never be able to convince her that this was a bad idea.

He took the deck of cards from his jacket pocket, shuffled them, and said, "Ladies and gentlemen, what I have here is an ordinary deck of cards . . ."

An hour later, Maisie and Felix had two dollars and twenty-five cents, and they were sitting in one of the wooden cars on the Ferris wheel, slowly rotating upward.

"You promised we could go on The Roundabout," Felix reminded Maisie.

They were standing on top of a giant wooden elephant called The Elephant Colossus. They'd already gone inside its legs. One had a cigar store and another sold postcards. The body of the elephant was a hotel, and here, twelve stories up, was an observation deck where they could look down on the runway, which throbbed with people.

Dusk had settled over Coney Island. The beach beyond the amusement park was still crowded. People splashed in the ocean beneath a reddish-orange sky.

"I know," Maisie said. "It's just hard to get enthusiastic about a merry-go-round."

"I went on The Serpentine Railroad with you," he said. "Three times."

The Serpentine Railroad was the other roller coaster that went all of twelve miles an hour, twice as fast The Gravity Pleasure Switchback Railroad but still eternally slow. Felix had started to enjoy the slower pace of the rides, how the Ferris wheel took almost twenty minutes to go around and the roller coasters felt like a ride in a convertible, the wind blowing on his face and the salt air of the ocean mixed with the smell of hot dogs roasting and the pungent oil they used to grease the tracks.

Those hot dogs. Felix had eaten three. And two Italian ices, sold by a man in a straw hat and red-and-white-striped jacket. He played a strange instrument that he told them was called a hurdy-gurdy. It had strings and a keyboard, and the man cranked it to make music that sounded almost like bagpipes. As he played it, a skinny little monkey with big eyes danced in front of him.

Thinking about it made Felix hungry again. He

smiled to himself. What a perfect day this had been. He had been careful not to mention the fact that they had no idea where Great-Aunt Maisie or Great-Uncle Thorne might be. Maybe they were out there somewhere in that crowd waiting in line to ride the Ferris wheel or to enter one of the sideshows. Maybe they were back in Newport at Anne Hutchinson Elementary School. Felix knew that if he speculated on their whereabouts with Maisie, she would get mad at him for ruining the day. He could almost hear her grumbling about those old people getting in the way of a perfect summer day at Coney Island.

Wait a minute, Felix thought. *A perfect summer day?*

"Maisie?" he said.

"Okay, okay, we'll go on the merry-go-round."

"Wasn't the Talent Show in March?" he asked her.

She narrowed her eyes at him. "That rhetorical question is supposed to make me realize something, right?"

Felix opened his arms wide. "It's definitely summer here."

"So?" she said.

She hated when he figured something out before

she did. What did it matter that the Talent Show was in March, and it was summer here at Coney Island in 18 . . . 18-whatever?

"Sir?" Felix said, turning to the man beside him. "What's today's date?"

The man laughed. "Why? Do you have an important engagement?"

"As a matter of fact," Felix said. "I kind of do."

The man furrowed his dark eyebrows. "It is June 18, 1893."

With slow, deliberate motions, the man pulled a very large pocket watch from his vest pocket.

"And," he added, "it is seven seventeen PM."

He wiggled his eyebrows and turned back to his conversation.

"How could we have traveled to a different day?" Felix blurted.

When he saw that Maisie still didn't understand, he said, "Every other time, we landed back on the same day, just a different year. We left Newport during the VIP Christmas party on December 9, and landed in China on December 9. But December 9, 1899. We left Newport on—"

"I get it," Maisie said, considering what this might

mean. "This time we traveled back to 18—"

"93," Felix said.

"But three months *later*," she said.

Felix nodded.

"What could that mean?" Maisie asked.

"I don't know. Maybe nothing. But I don't like it," he added.

"Something's different this time," Maisie said.

"Right," Felix said. "But what?"

O—⚡

The carousel at Coney Island was like nothing Maisie or Felix had ever seen before. They were used to the one in Central Park that moved at a dizzying speed with loud music blasting from it. Felix thought this one, The Roundabout, was like a piece of art. Each horse had a real horsehair tail. Painted white and frozen in midleap or prance, they each had a vividly colored mane—scarlet or bright yellow or midnight blue—and bridles in turquoise or purple trimmed with shiny fake jewels.

"Creepy," Maisie said, pointing to the mouth of one of the horses, which showed a mouthful of teeth.

"He's smiling," Felix said. In fact, they all had their teeth bared like that.

"Or grimacing," Maisie said, climbing on.

Still, she had to admit that it was kind of lovely to ride slowly around on one of these painted horses as the sky shifted from dusk to night and the lights of Coney Island came on, illuminating the rides and the people and the runway in bright white light.

Maisie even gave in and took a second ride on The Roundabout before claiming she'd had enough.

Off the carousel, walking with the crowd, Felix began to feel a little nervous. Now that it was dark, he realized they had no place to sleep for the night. Surely Coney Island shut down at some point. And then what would they do?

His thoughts were interrupted by a man trying to lure customers.

"Ladies and gentlemen! Anywhere else but in the ocean breezes of Coney Island, she would be consumed by her own fire! But you can see Little Egypt's electric gyrations here! Now!"

The crowd pushed forward toward the man, taking Maisie and Felix with it.

"Don't rush," the man warned as he took people's nickels. "There's room for everybody."

He laughed when Felix gave him two nickels.

"You'll grow up a little tonight, son," he said. "And so will your girl." He pronounced *girl* like *goil.*

"She's not my girl," Felix said. "She's my sister."

That made the man laugh harder. He waved them along, starting his spiel again.

"Anywhere else but in the ocean breezes of Coney Island . . ."

"What do you think Little Egypt is going to do?" Maisie whispered to Felix.

A teenage boy in front of them turned around, surprised.

"Why, she dances the kootch. Haven't you heard?"

"What's that?" Maisie said, thinking it sounded like some kind of terrible disease instead of a dance.

"The hootchie kootch!" he said, looking at her like she had come from another planet. Which, Maisie thought, she had in a way.

Music came on, both eerie and familiar. The crowd hushed.

Out came a woman in a belly dancer costume. She wore purple harem pants and a midriff blouse made of layers of sheer lavender with gold circles hanging from it. Her torso was exposed, and as she stood in the spotlight, she began a series of undulations, rolling her stomach like a snake. Men whistled and clapped, but Little Egypt's kohl-lined dark eyes staring out at them from above a veil betrayed no emotion.

"That's the hootchie kootch?" Felix whispered in Maisie's ear.

She suppressed a laugh. The belly dancers were better at the Middle Eastern restaurant on Downing Street they used to go to sometimes on Sunday nights.

"Lame," Maisie whispered back.

They made their way back out through the crowd. The night had cooled, and Maisie shivered in the ocean air.

"Here," Felix said, slipping off his tuxedo jacket.

Maisie let him put it around her shoulders.

"What time do you think this place closes?" she asked him, trying not to sound worried.

"Oh," he said casually. "Late. Real late."

She forced a smile. "Then let's go see another show."

The first marquee that caught her eye boasted a strong man inside.

"The strongest man in the world," she said. "How about that?"

Felix agreed.

Inside the stuffy room, a cloud of cigar smoke hung in the air. A man with big muscles, a tiny waist, and a red unitard stood on a small stage, grunting with great exaggeration. In one hand, he held a dumbbell with a big disc attached to it. The disc said 60 POUNDS in black letters.

"That's him, I guess," Maisie said.

"Shhh." The people in front of them hushed her.

The man held the dumbbell out straight and approached a blackboard. With his free hand he took a piece of chalk, put it in the dumbbell-holding hand, and lifted that chalk with much fanfare.

"So?" Maisie said. "He can hold a dumbbell and a piece of chalk in the same hand?"

She was promptly shushed again.

The strong man kept his arm extended and with a great flourish, wrote his name on the blackboard.

The crowd gasped and applauded. They didn't stop until he had taken several bows and left the stage.

When the lights dimmed, Felix asked Maisie if she wanted to find another show.

She shook her head.

Maybe something good is coming up next, she thought. Besides, walking outside in the cool air reminded her that soon enough they would need to find a place to stay. Something about night made everything seem worse. Already anxious thoughts were creeping into her mind. Where were the handcuffs? Where were Great-Aunt Maisie and Great-Uncle Thorne? What would happen—

The lights came back on, interrupting her thoughts.

"Ladies and gentlemen," the announcer shouted, "the Brothers Houdini and the"—here he lowered his voice and gave it a scary tone—"Metamorphosis."

Felix looked at Maisie, but her eyes were on the stage. The *Brothers* Houdini? He'd heard of Houdini, the greatest magician to ever live. In fact, Great-Uncle Thorne had talked about him when he'd given Felix the magic stuff. But he'd never heard of a brother.

"Houdini," Felix whispered to his sister.

She shrugged. "Who's that?"

Before Felix could answer, two young men came out onto the stage wheeling a trunk. One was short and stocky with bushy dark hair, and the other was tall and muscular and red haired. Both wore elaborate, bright silk costumes, and the shorter one held a loop of ropes.

The shorter one started to talk.

"I'm gonna tie my brother up with these ropes," he explained.

Maisie shuddered. *Brother* came out like *brudder* and *these* like *deese*. With an accent like that, this guy would never make it.

"Then I'm gonna put him in this here trunk. Then I'm gonna lock the trunk," he continued.

"The old switcheroo," Felix said.

Maisie looked confused.

"That's what Great-Uncle Thorne called a trick like this," Felix said.

"Shhh," said everyone in the row in front of them.

"Sorry," he said, turning red.

They watched the magician do as he'd said: tie up his brother, put him in the trunk, lock the trunk.

Next, he wheeled out a screen and placed it in front of the trunk.

"See, what's gonna happen here," he said, "is me and my brother are gonna change places, faster than youse can blink your eyes."

He stepped forward, his eyes seeming to pierce through the crowd.

"When I clap my hands three times," he said solemnly, "behold! A miracle!"

The magician stepped behind the curtain and clapped his hands loudly.

Once.

The audience craned their necks in unison.

Twice.

They held their breaths.

Three times.

Out from behind the curtain came the red-haired taller brother, who slid the curtain back, unlocked the trunk, and out came the other Houdini brother.

Stunned, the crowd did not utter a sound. They did not make a move. Silence covered the room.

"Metamorphosis," the dark-haired brother announced, lifting his arms in victory.

After a few more seconds of silence, the audience finally applauded.

The Brothers Houdini took their bows and left the stage.

Maisie and Felix watched as a family of sword swallowers took their places.

"Wait a minute," Felix said.

Even though he got hushed again, he couldn't be quiet. He grabbed his sister's arm so that she would be certain to hear what he had to tell her.

"The handcuffs," he said. "Houdini could escape from any handcuffs in the world. He was an escape artist."

Maisie let his words sink in.

Then she said, "Let's go."

"Go where?" Felix said, following her toward the exit.

"To find Harry Houdini," Maisie said.

CHAPTER 7

Harry Houdini

Surely the tall, red-haired brother was Harry Houdini, Felix decided as he and Maisie made their way to the back door where they'd been told the performers exited. That little guy had terrible grammar, and he looked so intense he scared Felix when his light-eyed stare seemed to briefly alight on him.

"If this Houdini guy is who we're supposed to find," Maisie said, pulling Felix's tuxedo jacket tighter around her, "we could give him the handcuffs right away and be back at Elm Medona by bedtime."

She added, "*If* we had the handcuffs."

They reached the back door, and the strong man was just coming out. Up close in the harsh light above the door, he looked much older. His lined face was covered in thick, orange pancake makeup, and he smelled like smoke.

"Excuse me," Maisie said to him. "Are the Houdini Brothers still in there?"

"Yeah, they're in there," he answered in a thick accent that sounded like Katya who worked at the Polish deli their father liked. "Practicing," he said, shaking his head. "Always practicing. Especially that Ehrich. The other one, Dash, he just goes along with him."

"Ehrich?" Felix said, confused. "Dash? There must be another Houdini brother then."

The strong man shrugged. "Maybe. Who knows? They live in Manhattan, up in the East Sixties. There might be a dozen Houdini brothers."

He waved good-bye with his large hand and walked away, getting swallowed up into the crowd of the amusement park.

Maisie turned to Felix.

"These are the wrong Houdinis!" she said. "Now what? Are we supposed to find some other Houdinis?"

"I don't know," Felix said, puzzled. "Maybe I was wrong and the handcuffs are supposed to go to someone else. It just seemed interesting that Great-Uncle Thorne told me about Harry Houdini and how he could escape from any pair of handcuffs *and* Great-Aunt Maisie was hiding these *and* we ended up at Coney Island at a magic show given by the Brothers Houdini *and—*"

"Okay, okay," Maisie said. "Everything adds up."

"Except who are Ehrich and Dash Houdini?" Felix asked.

"Actually, it's Dash Weiss," a deep voice said.

Felix and Maisie looked up into the blue eyes of Dash.

How long has he been standing there? Felix wondered. *What else has he heard us say?*

"You're not Houdini?" Felix said.

Dash laughed and stretched his hand out for Felix to shake.

"There is no Houdini," he explained. "Or, more accurately, Houdinis, since there's two of us. Ehrich read some book about a French magician, and he liked the name, that's all."

Maisie sighed. "So the guy we're looking for is in France then. How are we supposed to get to France?"

Dash laughed again, harder this time.

"You'll have to go farther than France if you want to meet Jean-Euge'ne Houdin," he said.

"Where is he?" Felix asked.

They'd sailed for weeks across the Atlantic with Alexander Hamilton and escaped the Boxer Rebellion in China with Pearl Buck. They would just have to do whatever it took to find the right Houdini.

"No matter where," Felix said. "We can do it."

"I don't think so," Dash said. "He died over twenty years ago. Unless you know a way to the afterlife."

He watched Felix's flummoxed expression.

"Ah," he said, "I didn't think so."

He began to walk away, still laughing to himself.

"Wait a minute!" Felix called after him.

Dash Weiss paused.

"But why are you and Ehrich the Brothers Houdini then?"

Dash shook his head. "Ehrich," he said. "He's obsessed with Jean-Euge'ne Houdin. He read his book, and he's learned some of his tricks, so now he's taken his name, too. Except his friend gave him the bright idea of adding the *i* at the end." He waved his hands in the air. "Sounds more mysterious."

Felix nodded.

"Well," he said, "thanks, anyway. Ehrich Houdini isn't the guy we're looking for, either."

"Maybe Ehrie can help you," Dash said. "If he ever stops practicing and comes out."

"Did you just call him Harry?" Maisie said, unsure if she'd heard right.

Dash grinned. "Ehrie," he corrected her. "That's his nickname. Like I'm Dash, but my name is really Theo."

"Oh," Maisie said, disappointed.

"But it's funny you say that. He calls himself Harry. For the act, you know. Sounds more American."

Maisie and Felix looked at each other and then back at Dash, who tipped his hat at them and disappeared in the darkness.

"Ehrich Weiss," Felix said, unable to contain his excitement. "He's Harry Houdini!"

The door burst open, and out stepped the man they were looking for. Harry Houdini, all five feet five inches of him, turned his blue-gray eyes onto first Felix and then Maisie.

"Youse guys need something?" he asked.

Felix broke into a big smile.

"In fact, Harry Houdini," he said, "we do."

To Maisie, Harry Houdini acted like a grown-up. Maybe it was his intense eyes that seemed to bore right through a person. Or maybe it was the confidence with which he moved and spoke, like he was already world famous. Even though she had never heard of Houdini, the fact that Felix had made Maisie look at him differently. With Clara and Alexander and Pearl, they didn't have any idea who they would grow up to be or what things they would do. But here was someone whose future they knew. And somehow, that made Maisie feel differently.

"Let me ask youse," Harry said. "Was the trick bad? Did it not amaze you?"

"The Metamorphosis?" Felix said, surprised. "It was awesome!"

"We did the switch in three seconds," Harry continued as if Felix hadn't spoken. "Do we need to be faster? *Can* we be faster?"

He slapped his forehead. "Ach!" he moaned. "Dash is incapable of being faster."

Harry sighed and shook his head. "The last time we tried to improve it, he forgot to take the . . ."

"Forgot to take what?" Felix asked eagerly.

As if he just remembered Maisie and Felix were standing there, Harry cleared his throat.

"Never mind about that," he said dismissively.

"You almost told us a trade secret," Maisie said.

Harry frowned at her. "Did you say you wanted something?"

"Uh, yes," Maisie began.

But Felix stepped forward, whipping the jacket from her shoulders as he did.

"We have something for you, Harry," he said.

"We do?" Maisie asked.

Felix reached into the jacket pocket and pulled out the handcuffs.

"You have them?" Maisie said, surprised.

"They're yours, I think," Felix said, handing them to Harry.

Harry took them and held them up to better examine them, nodding as he did.

"I've studied locks all my life," he said as he opened and closed the cuffs. "It's an obsession of mine."

He turned those light eyes on Maisie and Felix again. "I have photographic eyes," he said. "That's how I can remember how each type of handcuff works. And that's how I know how they can be opened."

"We want you to have these," Felix said. "For your act."

"And what's in it for you?" Harry said.

"For me? Nothing," Felix said, surprised.

Maisie said. "Actually, we could use a place to stay."

Harry narrowed his eyes. "Tonight?"

Felix nodded.

"No," Maisie said. "For maybe a few nights."

"Impossible," Harry said. "We got a job with a circus. In Ohio. We leave the day after tomorrow."

He handed the handcuffs back to Felix.

"That's okay," Felix said. "You can keep them."

Harry shrugged and put the handcuffs in his pocket. "Thank you," he said, almost reluctantly.

The three of them stood in awkward silence.

"You can come home with me," Harry finally said. "For tonight."

"Thank you," Felix said.

"Perhaps you can tell me more about The Metamorphosis," he said, his head bent as he began to walk toward the runway. "Why didn't the audience love it?"

Maisie and Felix fell in behind him.

"We've got to figure out a way to go to Ohio with him," Maisie said in a low voice.

"Right," Felix said, feeling that feeling he got when he didn't like the way things were going. One minute he was happily riding a carousel, and all of a sudden it looked like he was about to join the circus.

Maisie woke up early the next morning, just as the sun came through the slats of the Venetian blinds on the living-room windows. She stretched and wrinkled her nose. The Weisses' apartment smelled like the cabbage Mrs. Weiss had given them for dinner the night before. The cabbage tasted bitter, and the meat stuffed inside it didn't help any. Even though Harry claimed to be from Appleton, Wisconsin, his whole family had those accents like the people in that Polish deli.

After dinner, Harry had done magic tricks for everyone. Maisie winced, remembering the sight of him swallowing a handful of needles and some bright red thread, then pulling it all out of his mouth with every needle threaded. He'd stood there looking like he'd really accomplished something, but Maisie thought it was gross.

On the other hand, Felix looked like his eyes might literally pop out of his head. He'd stammered and stuttered praise, which Harry gobbled up. Harry Houdini was a total show-off, and even though Felix couldn't get enough of him and his gross tricks, Maisie was already completely sick of him.

That was why she had to figure out how to get back. Soon. But how could she make Harry give them a lesson?

She stared up at the cracks in the ceiling as if they might give her some clues. One looked vaguely like a rooster. But mostly they were just cracks in a ceiling that needed painting. Maisie sighed and began a mental list of all the problems she and Felix had.

Number one: They had time traveled three months later than when they left.

Number two: They had time traveled from the school auditorium instead of The Treasure Chest, something she hadn't realized they could do.

Here she added a note to herself to explore this

further when—if!—they got back home.

Number three: They had possibly lost Great-Aunt Maisie and Great-Uncle Thorne.

Only three items on her list, but to Maisie they seemed huge. Just when she thought she might be figuring out how this time travel thing worked, everything got turned upside down.

Maisie realized that Felix was awake, too, staring up at her from the mound of blankets on the floor where he'd slept. His cowlick was standing at attention, and he had crease marks on his face.

"Maisie," he whispered, his cabbagey morning breath hitting her in the face, "I just realized something."

She waited.

"We left from *school*," Felix said, looking worried. "I thought we had to be in The Treasure Chest. But we were just standing in the auditorium and—"

"No kidding," Maisie said, rolling her eyes. "I figured that out a long time ago."

"I mean, we could take an object with us and just go, any time we want," he continued.

"Irrelevant," Maisie muttered. "What we need to figure out now is how to get back."

"Well, we gave him the handcuffs," Felix said.

"Obviously," Maisie said.

Felix yawned.

"You need to brush your teeth," Maisie said crabbily.

"That cabbage was disgusting," Felix said. He opened his mouth and blew a blast of bad breath at Maisie.

"Ugh!" she groaned, pulling the blanket up over her mouth and nose.

Felix suppressed a giggle.

"You are *so* not funny," Maisie told him.

"Maisie?" he said. "Actually, I'm not in such a hurry to get back. I mean, his magic tricks are so great. Can you imagine if I could learn that needle and thread one?"

"Mom is not going to let you swallow needles," Maisie said. "No way."

"I don't think he really swallows them," Felix said, growing thoughtful. "He just makes us *think* he swallowed them. Magic is all about perception, you know. So he made us think he swallowed those needles, but how did he thread them like that?"

"I don't care how he did it," Maisie said. "Can you

stop trying to figure out how he did that stupid trick and use your brainpower to figure out how to get home?"

"Do you know what he told me?" Felix asked, ignoring her question. "He told me that he can hang upside down from a trapeze and pick up needles with his eyelids."

"That," Maisie said, "is ridiculous."

"With his eyelids!" Felix said again as if she hadn't heard it the first time.

Maisie rolled her eyes again. *What an idiot Harry Houdini is,* she thought.

No sooner did she have that thought than Harry himself strode into the living room, mumbling to himself. He was carrying a bunch of ropes and frowning at them.

Excited, Felix sat up.

"Morning, Harry!" he said.

Harry either didn't hear him or pretended not to hear him. He just kept mumbling and playing with those ropes.

"Working on a rope trick?" Felix asked.

He sounds like an eager puppy, Maisie thought.

Finally, Harry glanced up.

Felix grinned at him.

"Mebbe," Harry said.

"*May. Be,*" Maisie said. "Maybe. Not mebbe. Your English is atrocious."

She thought this would make him angry, but instead he nodded.

"I'm working on sounding better," he said. "Mebbe . . . *maybe* you can help me?"

"We're not sticking around long enough for that," Maisie said.

But Harry wasn't listening to her. He had started to run in place, moving his arms up and down in rhythm with his feet.

"Time for me to go exercise," he said. "We can discuss when I get back."

"I didn't say I would—" Maisie began.

Harry hardly noticed her as he jogged past her and Felix and out the apartment door.

"Discipline," Felix said. "That's how he does it. He even works out his toes."

"Oh, please," Maisie said.

Felix stared at the closed door, shaking his head.

"The Prince of Air," he said. "That's what they call him."

"That's what he calls himself," Maisie said. "Harry Houdini is nothing great, Felix. He's the Prince of *Hot* Air," she added. "Mebbe."

CHAPTER 8

Freaks and Geeks

"How can a circus not have any animals?" Maisie demanded.

She stood in a muddy field somewhere in Ohio, her hands on her hips, her eyes blazing with anger as she glared at Harry Houdini. Faded circus tents littered the field. In the gray afternoon light, Maisie could see how patched and frayed the tents were.

"This is the saddest-looking circus I've ever seen," she continued.

Harry smirked at her.

"You ain't no circus expert," he told her.

"Don't say *ain't*!" Maisie reprimanded.

Harry had only agreed to let Maisie and Felix accompany him and Dash to Ohio if Maisie promised to work on his grammar and pronunciation with him. They had fought the entire trip from New York to Columbus, sitting on uncomfortable wooden benches in the cheapest train car available.

Now that they had finally arrived, Maisie was even more miserable. The circus was really a group of performers that Harry called geeks and another group that he casually called freaks—a fat lady, a giant, a legless woman, and someone who Harry called the ossified woman.

"Ossified?" Maisie had asked him. "What is *ossified?*"

Harry had just shrugged. "Ya know, the skeleton woman."

"No," Maisie said. "I don't know."

"I think," Felix had offered, "*ossified* means something that has turned to bone."

"Right," Harry said smugly. "Emma Schiller is the Ossified Woman. She's like a skeleton."

"That is impossible," Maisie had said in disgust.

But now that they were actually here, she was afraid that there really might be a skeleton woman among all the other oddities in the show. She had already seen a woman covered with tattoos—more tattoos than Maisie had ever seen on one person—walking past with a woman with a beard. "That there's the Tattooed Lady and the Bearded Woman," Harry had pointed out.

Maisie narrowed her eyes.

"Harry," she said. "That sign says this is a museum."

"A dime museum," Harry said. "Right."

"A circus without animals and a museum without art," Maisie said.

"You ever heard of P. T. Barnum?" Harry asked.

"No."

"Yes, you have," Felix said. "Barnum and Bailey. The circus."

Maisie didn't realize the Barnum in Barnum and Bailey was a person. But she didn't want Harry to know that, so she nodded, pretending to remember that of course she knew all about P. T. Barnum.

"Oh, *that* P. T. Barnum," Maisie said. "What about him?"

"He started all this. The dime museums. In New York. The sideshow and the geeks, all for a dime," Harry explained. "People are calling it a circus these days, that's all."

Felix gasped and pointed to a figure walking toward them. *Well, not exactly walking,* Felix thought, staring harder. The woman had a normal head and body, but instead of legs, her feet were attached to her hips. She had no legs at all. Realizing that he was pointing, he quickly dropped his hand. But he couldn't stop gaping.

"What in the world . . . ?" Maisie said under her breath.

"That's Unthan," Harry said. "The Legless Wonder. She's one of the freaks," he added.

Maisie whipped around to face him. "Stop saying that!" she said angrily.

"Saying what?" Harry asked, surprised.

"Freaks," Felix said. "That's mean."

"But that's what they are," Harry said, his face washed with confusion.

"She has a birth defect," Maisie said. "She can't help how she looks."

Harry shrugged. "Who said it was her fault? She's a freak of nature. Good thing there's circuses so she can work, ya know? Make a living for herself."

Maisie shook her head. "Harry, people pay to stare at her. They probably make fun of her. That's wrong."

"No, Maisie," Harry said, growing frustrated. "You're wrong. People are amazed by what she can do. And you should see the Armless Wonder! She shuffles cards and deals them with her feet. She even holds a pen with her toes and—"

"Stop!" Maisie said. "I don't want to hear about it."

Felix, trying to make peace, quickly said, "It's okay, Harry. We just don't use the word *freaks*."

Harry looked at him, bewildered.

"We?" Harry asked.

"Uh . . . Maisie and me, I mean."

Harry laughed. "Then what do you call that?" he said, indicating the woman who had joined Unthan, the two of them talking together in the near distance.

Maisie blinked hard. Was she really seeing what she thought she was seeing?

"That's right," Harry said, folding his arms across his barrel chest. "Myrtle has four legs. She has half of another person growing out of—"

"Enough!" Maisie said, looking away from the poor woman.

"If you're going to travel this circuit with me," Harry said, "you're going to have to get used to the freaks, 'cause they ain't going nowheres."

With that, he headed off to the small train car that would be his and Dash's home for the next week.

"They *aren't* going *anywhere!*" Maisie called after him.

Harry turned around, grinning. "That's what I said!"

"Oooohhh," Maisie said through gritted teeth. "Harry Houdini drives me crazy."

All the performers lived in old train cars parked at the edge of the field. Each car had been divided into thirds, leaving a small, cramped, dark area for a living space. It just fit two narrow cots covered with scratchy gray blankets and yellowed sheets, and one flat, square pillow. The floor was covered with sawdust. Maisie and Felix slept on the other side of Harry and Dash's room, and they could hear Harry grunting as he did his push-ups and sit-ups early every morning.

Everyone ate together in a tent they called The Dining Room. Long wooden tables with benches filled the tent. One of them held the food: vats of scrambled eggs for breakfast, soup and bread for lunch, meat and potatoes for dinner. Felix liked mealtime. He liked the camaraderie of the performers, the easy way they spoke to one another, joking and teasing. After the evening shows, everyone gathered in The Dining Room, passing around a bottle of whiskey and telling stories until late at night.

Maisie quickly became friends with Felicity LaSalle. Felicity and her mother and little brother Francois had albinism, a condition that gave them chalk-white skin and chalk-white hair and pale pink eyes. When Maisie had first seen them at dinner, she'd had to look away. But Felicity LaSalle came up to her afterward and asked if Maisie and Felix wanted to play pick-up sticks with her and Francois.

"It's so good to have other kids here," Felicity said. Her pink eyes sparkled with hope as she added, "We could be friends, you and me."

It had been so long since Maisie had had a friend that Felicity's offer almost brought her to tears. Back in Newport, she had tried to become part of any of the groups of girls. But they had all known one another since preschool, and no one seemed interested in this odd kid from New York City. When her mother suggested she make friends with just one girl because that might be easier, Maisie had invited Hannah McGraw over after school. Like Maisie, Hannah was often alone. She didn't look weird or do anything strange, but she didn't really belong anywhere. Surely she would like a best friend, too, Maisie had thought.

Hannah McGraw came over one afternoon after school before Maisie and her family had officially moved into Elm Medona.

"My name is a palindrome," Hannah had announced as soon as they settled into the apartment's kitchen.

"It is?" Maisie asked, unsure what exactly that meant.

"Madam, I'm Adam," Hannah said.

"Um . . . what?" Maisie asked.

"A man. A plan. A canal. Panama," Hannah said.

Had her voice always been this flat and somehow I never noticed? Maisie wondered.

"The Panama Canal?" Maisie asked.

She remembered her mother's advice about small talk. *Listen carefully to what the person is saying and make a smart or witty comment about it to show you are interested.*

"We haven't studied that yet in social studies," Maisie said, struggling to think of something interesting to say on the topic. "But I know it's . . . um . . . in Panama . . ."

Hannah said, "Go hang a salami. I'm a lasagna hog."

The popcorn popped in the microwave. The bubbles popped in the glasses of ginger ale. Otherwise, there was no other sound. Until Hannah stood up and announced she was leaving.

"Thank you for the soda," she said, even though she hadn't taken one sip.

"The popcorn's ready," Maisie said, holding the steaming bag as evidence. She hated how desperate she was for a friend that she would try to make this weirdo stay longer.

"No thank you," Hannah said.

She frowned as if she was thinking hard.

"Elm Medona," she said after a moment. "Elm Medona is not a palindrome."

Maisie shrugged.

"Hannah," Hannah said in her strange, flat voice. "H-A-N-N-A-H."

"Okay," Maisie said.

"And backward. H-A-N-N-A-H."

"Oh!" Maisie said, finally getting it. "That go hang a salami thing is the same backward? Really?"

"Go hang a salami," Hannah intoned. "I'm a lasagna hog."

"That's pretty cool," Maisie said. She opened the bag of popcorn and offered it to Hannah.

"I don't like the kernels when they get stuck in my teeth," Hannah said.

Maisie put the bag of popcorn on the table beside the untouched glasses of ginger ale.

"Maybe it's an anagram," Hannah said.

"Maybe." Maisie said thoughtfully. She knew Phinneas Pickworth had loved anagrams. There was the one for the Fabergé egg, *Maisie Pickworth* all shuffled around. She would have to talk to Felix about figuring out Elm Medona's anagram.

Now, Maisie looked at Felicity's pale, hopeful face.

"I would like to be your friend," Maisie said.

Felicity smiled. She shook the wooden box she'd been holding, then turned it upside down, letting the colorful sticks fall onto the table.

O—➤

Later, after many games of pick-up sticks and Francois went off to bed, Felicity explained about albinism.

"It runs in families," she said softly. "My father didn't have it, though. He had dark, curly hair and dark brown eyes and beautiful olive skin."

"What happened to him?" Maisie asked, thinking of her own father.

"After I was born like this, and then Francois came along and was also an albino, he left," Felicity said sadly. "I don't really remember him. But I have this."

She reached into her pocket and pulled out a wrinkled sepia photograph of a man in a bowler hat. His dark eyes stared out at Maisie.

"My father left, too," Maisie said.

Felicity's white hand patted Maisie's.

"I can't see you until dinner tomorrow," she said. "We can't go out in the sun."

"I'm sorry," Maisie said.

"Sorry? For what?"

"I don't know. That you can't go out in the sun and that your father left and—"

"Don't be sorry," Felicity said. "It's just my bad luck."

After just a couple of days, Felix almost forgot that Myrtle had four legs or that Jojo stood only two and a half feet tall. They seemed like anybody else he knew and liked: funny, smart, and good storytellers. All of them were. One night as he lay on his cot, he wondered what their lives would be like if they didn't have the dime museums. How would they live? Who would hire Willy the Werewolf, for example, with his face completely covered in hair and his fanglike teeth? Maybe Harry was right.

But all of it disgusted Maisie. She hated how people paid a dime just to stare and point at them. Now that she and Felicity LaSalle were best friends, she hated that Felicity had to perform in something called a freak show. Felicity wasn't a freak. She had a genetic condition, that was all.

"They're like animals in a zoo," Maisie said. "It's wrong, wrong, wrong."

Felix felt confused about all of it. Like Maisie, he never went into the sideshow tents. Instead he spent the evenings watching sword swallowers and fire-eaters and, of course, Harry and Dash. But at meals and after shows, he sat with Willy and Unthan and Jojo—all of them—and enjoyed their friendship.

The next-to-the-last night before they were scheduled to leave Ohio, Maisie and Felix walked around the grounds as usual. And, as usual, a line of people for the sideshow snaked around the tent.

Maisie shuddered at the sight of all those people willing to pay dimes to gawk at her new friends.

She pointed to the sign hanging on the tent that shouted in big letters: FREAKS!

"Look at that," she said, disgusted.

Felix decided it might be time to share his theory with Maisie.

"I know," he said carefully. "It's terrible. But don't you kind of think that it's maybe okay?"

"Are you crazy?" Maisie said, looking at him like he had gone mad. "They have birth defects. They're not freaks. They're people with disabilities."

"But what would they do in the real world? Do you think they could get jobs driving buses or fixing things or—"

"I don't know," Maisie said. "That's not the point. The point is that all of these people are paying to stare at them and laugh."

"You don't know that," Felix said, his opinion starting to waver. "We've never gone inside. Harry said people were amazed by them."

"Amazed that someone has four legs or looks like a monkey or whatever. Not amazed by them as people," Maisie argued. "I bet they don't even realize they are people."

"Well," Felix said, "there's only one way to find out."

"Oh no," Maisie said. "I'm not going into anyplace that bills itself as a freak show."

"Well, I am," Felix said. "I want to see for myself exactly what goes on in there."

Felix headed for the back of the tent where the performers entered, Maisie on his heels.

But as he lifted the flap of the tent to enter, Maisie grabbed his arm and stopped him.

"I think it will upset us," she said quietly.

"Us?" Felix said.

"I'm not going to let you go in there alone," Maisie said.

They looked at each other for a moment.

It was so unusual for Felix to take charge like this that Maisie finally relented. In her heart, she knew it was a mistake to go inside. But she nodded her head, took her brother's hand, and lifted the flap of the tent to enter.

O━┳

Maisie and Felix joined the crowd of people waiting to enter the sideshow. To Maisie, the entire group seemed sweaty and disgusting. The air was heavy with the smell of that sweat mixed with cigar smoke and earth and animals from neighboring farms. She held her breath as long as she could, then took a few gulps of air. Felix hadn't let go of her hand. She watched him watching everyone, his eyes wide behind his glasses.

"Ladies and gentlemen," the barker shouted. "Come and view living monstrosities so horrible you very well may not sleep tonight. Were it not for an accident of birth, you might very well be like them. You, too, might have been . . ."

He paused, letting his eyes stop briefly on each face in the front of the crowd.

"A freak!"

All at once, the crowd moved. Maisie held on tight to Felix as they got pushed forward.

The first thing Maisie saw was the LaSalle family.

They sat together in a fake parlor pretending to play cards as if they weren't on display.

She watched as people stood, staring in horror, at the LaSalles.

"Zombies!" one woman screamed, burying her face in her husband's jacket.

Maisie pushed through the crowd.

"They aren't zombies," she said loudly. "They're just like you and me."

She caught sight of Felicity shaking her head no, but how could Maisie let this woman make fun of her friend?

"They have a genetic condition," Maisie continued. "Albinism."

"Out of the way, little lady!" someone yelled.

"Please," Felicity whispered. "Go away."

Maisie looked at her, surprised.

"But—"

Felicity made a shooing motion with her hands.

The crowd yelled for Maisie to get out of the way. Embarrassed and saddened, she let Felix pull her along.

In a small, empty space, Maisie could see how the sideshow was set up. The performers stood on little stages, each one acting as if all of these people weren't staring at them and heckling them. The Bearded Woman combed her beard. Willy the Werewolf paced back and forth, pounding his chest and grunting. The Armless Wonder wrote a letter, holding the pen with her toes. Frieda and Hans, the little people, were dressed as a bride and groom and sat in a miniature kitchen eating breakfast, even though in real life they didn't even like each other very much.

Felix and Maisie watched as people heckled their friends, laughed at them, or shivered in fear. Women covered their eyes with their hands and men taunted The Giant and Willy, poking them with their canes.

"Hey, freak," one man said to Unthan. "Can I touch your flippers?"

Without any expression, Unthan slid one of her feet toward him.

"Ew!" the man's wife said.

Maisie looked at Felix. "Had enough?" she asked him.

He nodded.

Together, they made their way back through the crowd and out into the warm night.

From another tent, Harry's voice announced the beginning of The Metamorphosis.

"Want to go watch?" Felix said.

"Okay."

In silence they walked into Harry's show, taking seats in the back. Felix tried to pay attention to the trick, but his heart felt too heavy to enjoy it. *What those people have to endure is not worth it at all*, he thought. Maisie was right.

As Maisie and Felix neared their room, Felix saw the LaSalles lugging a big trunk across the dirt.

"Hey! What are you guys doing?" he called to them.

Little Francois LaSalle stopped.

"Leaving," he said, his voice sounding very small in the dark, quiet night.

"Leaving? Now?" Felix asked him.

Francois nodded. "We got kicked out. Said we were trouble."

"Oh no!" Maisie said. "It's my fault!"

She ran across the muddy field to Felicity, whose red-rimmed eyes looked even redder than usual.

"I'll tell them it was my fault," Maisie said. "You didn't do anything wrong."

Mrs. LaSalle rested her hand on Maisie's shoulder.

"There's no use explaining to them, Maisie," she said. "They think we're troublemakers now, and there's no changing their minds."

"But where will you go?" Maisie asked desperately.

"Don't worry, darling," Mrs. LaSalle said. "There's dime museums all over the Midwest. We'll catch up with another one, maybe in Pittsburgh or Cleveland. They're always looking for freaks."

"But you aren't freaks!" Maisie insisted.

Mrs. LaSalle tousled Maisie's curls. "We'll be fine," she said.

The three LaSalles started off again.

"Felicity!" Maisie called.

Felicity turned to her.

"You're my best friend," Maisie told her.

Felicity grinned. "You're *my* best friend," she said, and then she blew Maisie a kiss before continuing on.

That night on her narrow cot, Maisie couldn't sleep. All she could think about was the LaSalles' fate. What would happen to them now? Where were they sleeping? How would they get all the way to Pittsburgh or Cleveland? She hated to think of her friend homeless, ridiculed, and afraid.

As soon as the first light of morning came through the small window, someone pounded on the door.

"It's Harry! Open up!" Harry shouted.

Maisie got up and let him in.

"Pack up," he said, smiling wide. "I just got booked at Tony Pastor's."

"Where's that?" Maisie said.

"Tony Pastor's New Fourteenth Street Theater. In New York City," Harry said. "We're going back home."

CHAPTER 9

Home at Last

Mrs. Weiss was not happy to see Maisie and Felix again. She frowned at them and muttered in whatever language she spoke, banging pots and pans onto the small stove.

"Mama," Harry said, throwing his arms around her, "are you making us your famous goulash?"

"To welcome you back home," she said, softening.

Two years earlier, when Mr. Weiss died, Harry had promised to take care of his mother. It was obvious to Maisie and Felix that Mrs. Weiss favored Harry. When he walked into a room, her usually stern face lit up.

"Maisie here is helping me with my enunciation, Mama," Harry explained. "And Felix is a magician, too."

Mrs. Weiss barely glanced at them. "Hah!" she muttered.

When the oil in the pan began to sizzle, Mrs. Weiss set about slicing onions and tossing them into the hot oil. She sprinkled a big amount of paprika on the onions and stirred. The little kitchen filled with the spicy aroma.

"That smells really good, Mrs. Weiss," Felix said.

"Ach!" she said dismissively as she took beef cubes from butcher paper. "Everyone out!"

Harry laughed. "Okay, okay, Mama," he said, kissing the top of her head. "We'll leave you to your goulash."

Out in the parlor, Maisie asked Harry where his family came from.

"Appleton, Wisconsin," he said.

"Harry," Maisie said, "your mother is not from Wisconsin. And neither are you."

Harry sighed. "Mama and Papa were born in Hungary, yes. In Pest. Papa was a very wise man. A rabbi."

"How did you get from Hungary to Wisconsin to here?" Felix asked.

"Papa followed work wherever it went," Harry said.

"Our father, too," Felix said, getting that sad feeling he got whenever he thought about how far away their father had moved. "He's an artist. A sculptor. But he took a job at a museum in Qatar."

"The Middle East," Maisie added.

"He'll send for you?" Harry asked. "When he gets settled?"

Felix shook his head. "We live with our mother."

"Families sometimes have to do this," Harry said matter-of-factly. "Separate in order to survive."

"Tell us how you got so good at magic," Felix said. He didn't want to talk about families separating. He didn't want to feel sad.

"When I was just nine years old, I learned to pick up needles with my eyelids, hanging upside down," Harry said, boasting. "I was the Prince of Air! And people paid to come see me in our backyard in Appleton. I loved to perform. And then one day, my father took me to see a magician named Dr. Lynn. Dr. Lynn's most famous trick was to cut up a man—"

"Cut him up?" Maisie said. "What do you mean?"

Harry made a chopping motion with his hands.

"Cut off an arm and a leg and even his head, then throw them all into a cabinet, close the curtain, and after a while, the man shows up, all in one piece. I watched that trick, and I knew I had to be a magician like Dr. Lynn. Better than Dr. Lynn!"

"You will be," Felix said.

"Ha!" Harry said. "I already am! I'm a magician and an escape artist, and now I'm working on cracking locks. All kinds of locks. This is an interest I've had my whole life, and I just keep getting better and better at it."

Mrs. Weiss laughed from the kitchen. "You learned to open locks just so you could get at my pies, Ehrie. That's what I think."

"Ain't that the truth," Harry said.

He glanced at Maisie. "I mean, *isn't* it?"

For half a second, Harry Houdini almost charmed her. *Almost.*

After the dinner of goulash and wide egg noodles followed by peach pie, Harry sequestered himself in his room to practice for his opening at Tony Pastor's the next night.

"Let's take a nice long walk," Maisie suggested to Felix.

They had tried to help Mrs. Weiss with the dishes, but she'd scowled at them and ordered them out of the kitchen.

It was a warm June night, and even with the windows open, the Weisses' apartment on East 69th Street felt stuffy and airless. A walk sounded like a great idea to Felix.

But once outside, Maisie grabbed his shoulders and, with her eyes bright with excitement, said, "Let's go see our old apartment."

Felix groaned. "Not again," he said.

When they'd held the coin and ended up following Alexander Hamilton from Saint Kitt's to New York City, Maisie had insisted that if they went to Bethune Street they might be able to figure out how to time travel forward enough to land smack into the time before their parents got divorced, when they'd all lived there together and been happy. But when they finally found the spot, Bethune Street was not even a street yet—it was under the Hudson River.

"Don't worry," Maisie continued. "I just want to see it, that's all."

"Really?" Felix asked, doubtful.

"Promise," Maisie said. "Besides, it's probably still underwater."

Felix let himself picture their old apartment. He imagined the kitchen with the old six-burner stove their father had salvaged and repaired as a gift for their mother. And he pictured his mother at that stove, stirring spaghetti sauce and humming a song from an old Broadway show. He could see his father's bike hung on the wall in the entryway, and the clutter of their rain boots and Rollerblades and sneakers beneath it. The way those shoes mingled, with Felix's laces tangled in his father's and Maisie's rain boots tucked into their mother's Wellies, anyone would know a family lived there.

"Okay," Felix said.

His mouth had gone dry, and the word came out like a croak.

"Now let's see," Maisie said, "we just have to get to the subway at Lexington Avenue and Fifty-Third Street."

"I don't think so," Felix said.

"You think we should walk over to Broadway instead?"

"Maisie, think about it."

"You want to walk over to Eighth Avenue?" Maisie said, turning west. "Fine with me."

"Maisie, it's 1894," Felix said. "There are no subways yet."

Maisie stopped in her tracks.

She couldn't imagine New York City without subways. One rainy Saturday, their father had taken them to the Transit Museum. They'd sat in old subway cars and saw the different ways fares had been collected, like the first paper ticket-choppers and the later turnstile designs that accepted coins and tokens. But she couldn't remember exactly when subways had started.

"Granville T. Woods," Felix said. "Invented the third-rail system for conducting electric power to railway cars. Without it, we wouldn't have had subways at all."

"Sounds vaguely familiar," Maisie mumbled. She hated when Felix knew more than she did.

"And as it is, *we* don't have subways at all right now. I think they're about ten years away."

"So we . . . walk? Sixty blocks?" Maisie did some fast calculating. Over three miles.

"No," Felix said. "We take one of those."

He pointed upward at an elevated train track with a train clacking along it.

"I suppose it's as easy as finding one going downtown," he said.

It was that easy. Twenty minutes later, Maisie and Felix were crossing Fourteenth Street and heading down Hudson Street. When they reached the corner of Hudson and Bethune, Maisie literally jumped with joy.

"We're home, Felix!" she said, clapping her hands.

Felix stood still, taking in everything around them. It looked the same, but it also looked completely different. Instead of cars moving up Hudson Street, there were carriages pulled by horses. And the smell of horse manure was almost suffocating in the summer air. Felix could actually see piles of it everywhere.

"Look, Felix," Maisie said, pointing down Hudson.

On the corner, two blocks away, stood the White Horse Tavern, right where it stood when they lived in the neighborhood. It looked exactly the same, too, just the way it looked when their father went there after work on Friday nights.

"Wow," Felix said.

He glanced down their block. The corner where a D'Agostino's supermarket should stand now had an apartment building on it instead.

"No D'Ag's," Maisie said as if she'd read his mind. "But it's the same building!" she realized.

"You're right," Felix said.

He took a deep breath and started down their block, Maisie walking close beside him.

"I don't know why, but I feel kind of creepy," Felix said.

They stopped in front of 10 Bethune Street.

"It looks the same," Maisie whispered.

His mouth had gone all dry again so Felix just nodded.

"If we go around the corner, and you stand on my shoulders, you can look inside our apartment," Maisie said hopefully.

"Well," Felix managed, "we've come this far. Might as well."

They rounded the corner onto Greenwich Street. A light shone in the window of what would have been their living room.

"I guess someone's home," Maisie said.

"Kneel down," Felix told her.

Maisie kneeled as close to the window as she could get, and Felix climbed onto her shoulders. The apartment seemed lower to him. But maybe he had grown in the almost year since he'd last been on Bethune Street.

Felix pressed his face to the window and peered inside.

"Do you see anything?" Maisie asked him, trying hard to stand steady.

"You won't believe it," Felix said.

"A family?" she asked, hoping he didn't see that.

"Hardly," he said, hopping off her shoulders.

She waited.

"Our apartment," Felix announced, "is a bakery."

"A what?"

"Yup. There's a row of big ovens and all kinds of baking stuff. I saw giant burlap bags of flour in there, and sugar and salt."

"No kids? No beds or—"

"It's a bakery," Felix said firmly.

"I like that," Maisie decided.

A bicycle came screeching to a halt beside them, almost knocking Felix down.

"Hey!" Maisie yelled at the kid on the bike. "Watch where you're going!"

She glared at him, but the boy gave her a giant smile.

"Aha!" he said. "I figured you'd show up here sooner or later."

Felix studied the boy's face.

"I know you," he said thoughtfully.

But even as he said it, he knew it was ridiculous. How could he know a kid—or anyone—in 1894?

The kid wasn't listening to him, though.

"I went up to the Weisses'," he said. "But they said you'd all gone off to Pennsylvania—"

"Ohio," Maisie corrected.

"Okay, Ohio," the boy said. "Then I saw the sign over at Tony Pastor's, and I knew you'd be back any day now. I thought, *Where will those two end up?* And then I thought, *They'll want to see their crummy little apartment over on Bethune Street.* And I was right."

That voice, Felix thought. More than that voice, that *attitude*. So familiar.

"Wait a minute," Maisie said. "How do we know you?"

Before the kid could answer, that photograph on the wall going up the Grand Staircase in Elm Medona flashed through Felix's mind. Great-Aunt Maisie posing for the camera, and Great-Uncle Thorne sticking his face in the picture.

This was that same face.

"Great-Uncle Thorne!" Felix managed.

The kid clicked his heels and bowed.

"One and the same," he said. "One and the same."

CHAPTER 10

Great-Uncle Thorne Explains

If there was one thing Maisie knew for certain—and right now, she did not feel certain of very much—she knew this neighborhood. She knew how the Mexican restaurant on the corner kept Christmas lights up all year and how the little café used barrels for tables; she knew that a few blocks north, where she and Felix and the somehow teenage Great-Uncle Thorne walked, fancy clothing boutiques lined the street. Except instead of fancy boutiques selling ridiculously high heels and tiny, wispy dresses, slabs of meat hung from hooks, dripping blood onto the streets. The air reeked with an iron-like smell combined with the odor of raw meat and sweat.

"Slaughterhouses," Great-Uncle Thorne said when he saw the look of disgust cross her face. "This is the Gansevoort Market, home to over two hundred slaughterhouses."

Felix gulped the fetid air, trying not to gag.

"Also home to the best steak and eggs in the city," Great-Uncle Thorne said, leading them past cow carcasses and pig heads and large strips of who knew what other kinds of meat.

Even when they ducked into a tiny restaurant, the smell followed them.

Felix glanced around the crowded place. Men in blood-splattered aprons shoveled huge amounts of steak and eggs into their mouths. It seemed they all knew one another, and their loud conversations made the place practically buzz.

Great-Uncle Thorne ordered three plates, then squeezed into the corner table with them.

"I don't understand," Maisie said as soon as he sat down.

He raised his eyebrows at her.

"How . . . ," she began, but she stopped because there were so many things she didn't understand, she wasn't sure what to ask first.

"How did I get here?" Great-Uncle Thorne asked.

"That we can figure out," Felix said. "At least, I think we can figure it out," he added.

Great-Uncle Thorne leaned back in his chair and surveyed them.

"You don't know very much about how all this works, do you?" he asked. He had to practically shout to be heard over the din of noise there.

Felix shook his head.

But, insulted, Maisie said, "We know how it works. We need a shard from the Ming vase. I guess we don't actually have to be *in* The Treasure Chest, but we both need to touch the object."

Satisfied, she smirked at Great-Uncle Thorne.

"Ha!" he said. "Just as I thought. You don't know anything about it."

"Well," Felix said, "we don't know how you can be here as a . . . a . . ."

"Young man?" Thorne said, smiling wickedly.

"Right," Felix said.

Great-Uncle Thorne—it was hard to still think of him this way now that he was a teenager—leaned closer to them.

"You don't know why The Treasure Chest exists, do you?"

Without waiting for an answer, he continued. "You don't know why you two can do it when, for example, your parents couldn't. Or why Maisie and I can do it, do you?"

Again, he kept talking before they could answer. *Rhetorical questions*, Felix thought.

"You don't know why Maisie kept those handcuffs all these years or why she's been trying to get back here, do you?"

"All right!" Maisie said angrily. "Fine. We don't know any of that. So why don't you tell us?"

Just then, a man with massive arms rippling with muscles and covered with tattoos slid three heaping plates of food onto their table. He slapped down three cups of black coffee, splashing as he did. He grunted something at them, then walked away.

Great-Uncle Thorne cut into his bloody steak with delight.

"Bon appétit!" he said.

Felix stared down at the steak, blood oozing from it. His stomach flipped.

"Excuse me," he called to the man who had brought them the food.

The man stopped and glared at him.

"I like my steak well done," Felix said.

"That is done well," the man said gruffly.

"No," Felix said. "This is rare." He held up a bloody piece of steak as evidence.

The man threw back his head and laughed heartily. "Rare?" he managed to say. "Hardly, my boy. The streets are full of beef. It ain't at all rare."

"I mean, it's cooked rare."

"Whatever you say, son," the man said, wiping at his eyes and walking off. "Whatever you say."

The eggs, which Felix didn't like, either, had blood seeping into them. He pushed the plate away and tried to focus on what Great-Uncle Thorne, who was chewing away happily, was about to tell them instead.

"So tell us," Felix urged. "Why can we do it?"

"Why do you think?" Great-Uncle Thorne said between bites.

"Because we live in Elm Medona?" Maisie guessed.

"Irrelevant!" Great-Uncle Thorne announced.

"Because we're related to Phinneas Pickworth?" Felix said.

"Closer," Great-Uncle Thorne said.

"You're just like Great-Aunt Maisie," Maisie grumbled. "She can never tell us anything. She always makes us figure it out."

Great-Uncle Thorne's blue eyes glistened. "That's how we were raised. Our father loved puzzles and games, anagrams and mysteries."

"Well it's not fun," Maisie told him. "It's frustrating."

"Twins!" Felix said suddenly. "We're twins. And you and Great-Aunt Maisie are twins."

"Aha!" Great-Uncle Thorne said. "You've got it. You need twin power to time travel."

Maisie and Felix waited while he wiped up some egg with a hunk of bread and took a bite, which he chewed slowly.

Finally, he patted his mouth with a napkin, took a satisfied breath, and said, "My father, Phinneas Pickworth, and his twin sister, Amy, grew up time traveling. As did their father, Thaddeus, and his twin sister, Isabel. *All* Pickworth twins have done it."

"That doesn't make sense," Maisie said, shaking her head.

Great-Uncle Thorne looked at her, surprised.

"There's only two shards missing from the vase," Maisie said. "You can't do it without a shard."

Thorne waved his hand at her like she was a fly he was shooing.

"From *this* vase," he said. "The original Treasure Chest, and everything in it, was destroyed when the original Elm Medona burned down before Maisie and I were born."

"What?" Felix said. "There was another Elm Medona?"

Great-Uncle Thorne nodded. "The cottages used to be made of wood. Many of them burned down."

"It was in Newport, too?" Maisie asked.

Great-Uncle Thorne nodded again. "My father spent years traveling the world for objects to put in our Treasure Chest. Including replacing the Ming vases. He led an expedition through China searching for their matching twins."

"Twins," Felix said softly.

"Fine," Maisie said. "But what I want to know is how you can be sitting here and only be sixteen years old? When we were standing in the auditorium at school, you were old."

At that, Great-Uncle Thorne's face grew worried.

"Yes," he said. "This is all my sister's fault. If I ever see her again—"

"Then she's not with you?" Felix said.

"I haven't seen her," Great-Uncle Thorne said. "I was hoping you two had."

"But where could she be?" Felix said, panicking.

Great-Uncle Thorne sighed a deep sigh. "She's had this plan for decades."

"What plan?" Maisie asked.

"Many, many years ago," Great-Uncle Thorne said, "we picked up that pair of handcuffs in The Treasure Chest and landed here. In fact, we landed at Coney Island."

"That's where *we* landed," Felix said. "Didn't you?"

"I did," Great-Uncle Thorne said. "Smack on the midway. Thought I broke my hip. I lay there staring up into the face of a woman who looked quite worried. 'Young man,' she said. 'Are you all right?' I glanced left, then right, trying to see this young man of whom she spoke. She leaned closer to me. 'Young man?' she said, and that's when I knew it was me to whom she referred. *I* was a young man." He said this last with a sense of awe.

"But Great-Aunt Maisie?" Felix asked.

"By the time I got up and the woman inspected me and pronounced me fit to walk, Maisie was nowhere in sight." His jaw set with determination. "Of course I hightailed it straight to that rapscallion's show, certain I would find her there. But she seems to have vanished."

"Rapscallion?" Maisie said.

Great-Uncle Thorne narrowed his eyes. "Harry Houdini," he said as if it pained him to utter the name.

"But that's where we've been!" Felix exclaimed. "We've been staying with his family, and we went with him and his brother to Ohio and—"

"Stop!" Great-Uncle Thorne shouted.

Everyone in the restaurant went silent.

Great-Uncle Thorne stood, slamming his fists on the table.

"I *hate* Harry Houdini!"

After they calmed Great-Uncle Thorne down and left the restaurant with him, Maisie dared to ask why he hated Harry Houdini with such a passion.

"I'm not crazy about him, either," she said. "He

thinks he's the greatest thing ever, and he says *youse* and *ain't,* and he's obsessed—"

"You don't have to tell me about Harry Houdini," Great-Uncle Thorne said through gritted teeth. "I know all about him."

The three of them had walked uptown for several blocks, and slowly the smells of blood and meat were replaced with the wonderful aroma of baking bread.

Felix looked at the redbrick building in front of them. He blinked to be sure he saw what he thought he saw.

Satisfied, he forgot all about Great-Uncle Thorne and Harry Houdini and grabbed his sister's shoulder.

"Look!" he said, pointing. "We're at the Chelsea Market!"

Maisie broke into a smile. For a moment, this felt like *her* New York. The Chelsea Market was where they would go with their parents to buy specialty foods like good extra virgin olive oil and fresh fish.

But her smile disappeared as she read the sign: National Biscuit Company.

"Nothing's the same," she said sadly.

"Of course it isn't," Great-Uncle Thorne snapped at her. "You don't travel back in time to keep everything the same."

That reminded Felix of what they had been talking about a few minutes earlier.

"Why do you hate Harry Houdini so much?" he asked Great-Uncle Thorne.

"Because he and Maisie fell in love, that's why. When we came here all those years ago, they fell in love, and Maisie wouldn't come home with me. She said she was going to stay in 1894. With Harry. Even though she knew what happens if you stay . . ."

Maisie remembered her own desires to stay with Clara and Alexander. "What happens?" she asked.

Great-Uncle Thorne looked at her hard.

"You die. In the present."

Felix gasped.

"Now you understand why I had to do what I did. When we got back to Elm Medona, I took the shard and hid it from her—"

"She was right!" Maisie said. "You did steal it."

"Steal it?" Great-Uncle Thorne roared. "I hid it so she wouldn't go back. And she kept the handcuffs with the hope of finding an opportunity to return.

Without me and the shard, she was stuck. Until you two came along."

"Wait a minute," Felix said. "How did you get back if Harry didn't keep the handcuffs?"

"I knew you didn't know how any of this works," Great-Uncle Thorne said triumphantly. "Haven't you had any aborted missions yet?"

Maisie and Felix both shook their heads.

"You're lucky," Great-Uncle Thorne said. "It can happen. Some kind of wrinkle, and you never find your subject—"

"Subject?" Felix asked.

"The person who gets the object."

"So that can happen?" Maisie said. She'd been afraid of that.

"Very rare," Great-Uncle Thorne said. "But possible. I had to keep those handcuffs away from Harry and devise a way for Maisie and me to both touch them so that we could get home." He sighed at the memory. "Of course she's never forgiven me. And now, if Harry gets those handcuffs—"

"But he has them," Felix said. "We gave them to him."

"Oh no!" Great-Uncle Thorne said. "If Maisie

gets to Harry before we get those handcuffs back, then she'll stay here with him."

"But how will *we* get home then?" Felix asked.

He didn't like this at all. His mind swirled with all the information Great-Uncle Thorne was giving them. Was Great-Aunt Maisie really trying to stay in 1894 with Harry? And if she managed to do that, did that mean in the present, back home in Newport, she would die?

"The same way we always get back," Great-Uncle Thorne was saying. "When Harry gives us our lesson, we can't help but return."

Maisie considered what Thorne had just said.

"Yes, Clara is the one who told us to listen to Great-Aunt Maisie," she said.

"And Alexander told us to appreciate our parents," Felix added.

"And remember how we were fighting when we were in China with Pearl?" Maisie continued.

"Then she told us about losing her sisters and brothers and . . ."

He didn't need to finish. Maisie was already nodding.

"We need to get those handcuffs from Harry,"

Felix said. "Because we can't stop Harry from telling us anything."

"All he does is tell us stuff," Maisie said.

"Where is he now?" Great-Uncle Thorne said.

"At home, I guess," Felix said.

"On East 69th Street?" Thorne said.

As usual, he didn't wait for an answer.

"Let's get to the Weisses' apartment," he told them.

"Great-Uncle Thorne?" Maisie asked.

"We don't have time to waste," he growled.

"Just one question," Maisie said. "I still don't understand why you're here and twelve years old."

"Adults can't do it," he said. "If Maisie had tried to come back with just me, it wouldn't have worked. We needed to be with you two to even time travel. And I guess we not only traveled back to 1894, but we traveled back to our own younger selves."

He smiled wistfully.

"I have to admit," he said, "it feels wonderful."

Felix's mind raced with still more questions. But Great-Uncle Thorne didn't waste any more time in reflection. He started walking uptown, fast. And Maisie and Felix hurried along with him. There was too much at stake to dawdle.

CHAPTER 11

Tony Pastor's New Fourteenth Street Theater

The Weiss apartment was dark when Maisie, Felix, and Great-Uncle Thorne finally arrived back there. But already in the eastern sky, Felix could see the sun starting to come up. Soon Harry would be awake, doing his push-ups and sit-ups and what he called calisthenics. Harry had told Felix that he believed the thing that would make him famous someday was his self-discipline. "My fingers aren't mere fingers," he proclaimed. "They are superfingers! My toes can act like fingers. Why, I have trained myself to eat with my left hand as well as I can with my right." He practiced holding his breath, adding seconds each day. Then he went outside and ran, timing himself with a big stopwatch. Felix had never seen anyone as disciplined. "Be confident, be disciplined. To be great," Harry had told him one morning, "youse gotta act great."

Lying on the living room floor with Thorne snoring beside him, Felix tried to absorb all the information he'd learned tonight. But as soon as he began to go over what Great-Uncle Thorne had told them, panic overtook him. Great-Aunt Maisie was here somewhere. And if they didn't stop her, she would stay in 1894 with Harry, and when they got home . . . Here, Felix stopped himself. He didn't want to think about Great-Aunt Maisie dying or about any of the things that Great-Uncle Thorne had warned about.

Felix tossed and turned until he heard Harry get up and start moving around the kitchen. First Harry made his usual breakfast of a dozen eggs scrambled with a quart of milk. He believed eggs and milk made a person stronger. Then Felix listened to him begin his calisthenics, the floor shaking slightly with his movements.

Eventually, Harry came into the living room. Running in place, he stared down at Felix.

"Want to time me?" he asked.

Felix did.

Harry stopped running. After he gave Felix the stopwatch, he stood perfectly still, his eyes set with concentration. He took one deep breath, then another, before nodding at Felix to begin.

Felix started the stopwatch.

Harry's eyes were closed, his barrel chest puffed with air. Felix stared at him, marveling at his focus. *Nothing can distract him*, Felix thought. *Nothing.*

The hands of the stopwatch counted down thirty seconds.

Harry remained still as a statue.

One minute.

Felix thought about swimming at the Carmine Street Pool, how he and Maisie used to take turns trying to stay underwater the longest, eventually one of them popping up, sputtering for air.

Ninety seconds.

Ninety-one . . . ninety-two . . .

Felix saw a muscle in Harry's cheek twitch.

Ninety-six . . .

Harry's left eyelid quivered.

Ninety-nine . . .

Harry's eyes flew open, and he gulped air.

"Well?" he asked hopefully.

"One hundred seconds," Felix announced.

Harry's face drooped with disappointment.

"Ach!" he said.

"That's really good, Harry," Felix insisted.

But Harry shook his head. "Not for what I want to do," he said.

"What do you want to do, Harry?"

Harry's eyes grew dreamy. He looked off at a spot that only he could see.

"So many things, Felix," he said finally.

"Like what?"

"I am imagining escaping from a chest underwater. Like The Metamorphosis, but in the water. Maybe in the Hudson River."

"I don't know," Felix said. "That sounds really dangerous."

Even though Felix knew Harry would become maybe the best magician who ever lived, he wasn't sure how he got that fame. Did he escape from a locked chest under the Hudson River? Was that even possible?

"Not if I practice," Harry said. "It's all about discipline. Physical discipline and mental discipline."

"To be great," Felix began.

Hearing his own words, Harry laughed. "Correct," he said. "I want to be Prince of Air, King of Handcuffs, Emperor of—"

"Handcuffs!" Felix blurted.

Harry looked at him, confused.

"Harry, you know those handcuffs we gave you back on Coney Island?"

"Sure," Harry said.

"Since you already figured out how to open them, I was thinking maybe I could get them back? You know, so I can practice," Felix added quickly.

"No problem," Harry said.

Relief washed over Felix. Harry would give him the handcuffs, and they would be back in Newport in no time.

"Except," Harry continued, "I don't know where they are."

"What?" Felix said.

"Do you know how many sets of handcuffs I have?"

Too upset to speak, Felix just shook his head.

"I don't know, either! I've been studying every model I can find. There aren't so many differences,"

Harry said as if this fact disappointed him. "Some open with a sharp rap, some need a pin, some—"

"But I need that set," Felix interrupted.

Harry shrugged. "There's a pile of handcuffs in my room. You're welcome to find yours."

Jogging in place again, Harry wiggled his fingers in a wave, then moved across the floor and out the apartment.

Beside Felix, Great-Uncle Thorne popped up from his blankets.

"Well," he said, "no time to waste."

Great-Uncle Thorne pulled Felix to his feet.

"We've got to find those handcuffs. Now," he said. "Before Maisie finds *him*."

Two hours later, Great-Uncle Thorne and Felix sat bleary-eyed in front of a pile of handcuffs. They had examined each set, trying to determine which one was the set Maisie and Felix had given Harry. But despite minor differences—some were shinier than others, the chains connecting each handcuff came in varying lengths and widths, there were heavier ones and thinner ones—to Great-Uncle Thorne and Felix they all looked pretty much the same.

Defeated, Felix finally admitted that he had no idea which set was the right set.

When Maisie wandered in, her eyes still puffy with sleep and her hair a bedhead tangle, Great-Uncle Thorne immediately thrust several sets of handcuffs in her face.

"Are any of these the ones you gave him?" he demanded.

Maisie pushed the handcuffs away.

"You have to remember," Great-Uncle Thorne said.

"I didn't know there were so many kinds until right now," Maisie said, eyeing the pile. "They all look kind of the same, don't they?" she said.

"I think so," Felix said, his voice catching.

"There must be a solution," Great-Uncle Thorne said. He paced the length of the small room, past the piles of ropes twisted into various knots and the trunk and all the various locks and bright costumes.

"I know!" Great-Uncle Thorne said brightly.

He walked back to the heap of handcuffs and began to scoop them into his arms, the metal clanking noisily.

Felix and Maisie watched him, bewildered.

"Well?" Great-Uncle Thorne said. "What are you waiting for? Help me."

"What exactly are you doing?" Maisie asked him.

"Taking all of them," he said, exasperated. "Obviously."

When Maisie and Felix still didn't start to pick them up, Great-Uncle Thorne glared at them.

"Don't you see?" he said. "For all these years, I endured my sister's wrath just to protect her. To keep her alive. I can't lose her now because we can't find the thing that will save her. I can't."

Without any hesitation, Maisie and Felix gathered the remaining handcuffs.

"Thank you," Great-Uncle Thorne said, just as Harry boomed from the doorway.

"What do you three think you are doing? Put those down! Now!"

Harry would not budge.

"I need them for my act," he answered every time they tried to get him to relinquish the handcuffs.

"We'll give them back when we figure out which set is ours," Maisie said.

"Look," Harry told her, "I open at Tony Pastor's

tonight. I need to do my handcuff act. I'm famous for it."

Great-Uncle Thorne sniffed. "Famous? Hardly."

"And who exactly are you?" Harry demanded. "These two characters I know. But where did you come from?"

"I am the son of Phinneas Pickworth, grandson of Thaddeus Pickworth of Washington Square," Great-Uncle Thorne said in his haughtiest voice. *Which is pretty haughty*, Felix thought.

"Yeah, well I'm the son of Mayer Weiss, learned man and rabbi, of Appleton, Wisconsin, and I says youse can't have my handcuffs," Harry said, pulling himself up to his full five feet five inches.

Even at twelve years old, Thorne Pickworth towered over Harry.

"Really?" Great-Uncle Thorne said. "I believe that you are from Pest, Hungary, and *not* Wisconsin. In fact," he added, "I believe that you are a liar, Ehrich Weiss."

"Get outta here!" Harry yelled, his high voice turning to a screech. "All of youse!"

But Great-Uncle Thorne didn't budge. "Prince of Air, my foot," he said. "You put on a pair of red stockings, hung from a tree, and called yourself the Prince of Air."

"I was in a traveling circus," Harry insisted. "I was a trapeze artist, and I picked up needles with my eyelids, you . . . you . . ."

"You fraud!"

"You snob!"

"You prevaricator!"

At this, Harry balked. He blinked several times. Then he pointed his finger toward the door.

"Out," he said. "Now."

"Harry," Felix began.

But Harry shot him a look that made Felix shiver.

"Harry," Maisie tried, "if we could just keep the handcuffs for one night . . ."

The look on his face made her give up.

Great-Uncle Thorne, Felix, and Maisie left the apartment with Harry on their heels, making sure they went down those stairs and out the door. From behind them, they heard the Weisses' apartment door slam shut, hard.

"Great," Felix said as they stood on the sidewalk in front of 305 East 69th Street. "Now we don't have *any* of the handcuffs, no place to stay, and Harry is so mad at us he'll probably never talk to us again."

"I don't care about Harry Houdini," Great-Uncle Thorne roared. "We need to find my sister and keep her away from him."

Great-Uncle Thorne turned an icy stare on Maisie and Felix.

"It's a matter of life and death," he intoned.

"Then let's stop standing around and find her," Maisie said.

"I thought she would come here," Great-Uncle Thorne admitted. "She knows he lives here, after all."

"But she knows you know that," Maisie said. "She's going to try to outsmart you."

"Maybe she's on Coney Island," Felix said, warming to the idea of spending another day there in the sunshine, riding a slow roller coaster and letting the waves wash around his feet. Yes, he decided. That was much better than being here with Great-Uncle Thorne.

Great-Uncle Thorne considered this.

"We could split up?" Felix said hopefully. "Maisie and I could go to Coney Island to look for her and you could stake out the apartment."

"Hmm," Great-Uncle Thorne said. "Maybe."

"Actually," Maisie said, "isn't she safe as long as Harry doesn't teach us something?"

Great-Uncle Thorne's eyebrows bobbed. They were remarkable eyebrows for a twelve-year-old, bushy and expressive.

"That's how we get back, right?" Maisie said. "We give the item, and they give us a lesson."

"Oh no," Felix said, remembering all the advice Harry had given him already: *Be confident, be disciplined. To be great, youse gotta act great.*

"What?" Maisie demanded. "What did he tell you?"

"I don't know," Felix said. "Lots of stuff."

"Magic tricks don't count, do they?" Maisie asked Great-Uncle Thorne.

But Great-Uncle Thorne seemed to be already thinking of something else.

"No, no," he said. "Of course not."

"How about tips on how to succeed?" Felix asked miserably.

"He would of course have to give them to both of you," Great-Uncle Thorne said, still disinterested.

"Well," Felix began.

"Did that charlatan say he was opening at Tony

Pastor's tonight?" Great-Uncle Thorne said.

"Tony Pastor's New Fourteenth Street Theater," Maisie said.

"Oh, I know it well. That is the scene of all the unpleasantness. Dash had left the show, and Maisie and Harry decided to run off together after he did his act at Tony Pastor's. That's when Maisie and I had the fight, and I orchestrated our return." Great-Uncle Thorne's whole demeanor seemed to wilt with sadness at the memory.

Aha! Maisie thought. Now she understood why they'd traveled back to June instead of March.

"We're redoing your time travel here, aren't we?" she said.

Great-Uncle Thorne suddenly brightened. "Why, yes, I believe we are."

"Huh?" Felix said.

"My sister and I landed on Coney Island on June 18 the first time. And that's when we landed this time as well," Great-Uncle Thorne said, nodding as he spoke.

"I get it!" Felix said. "Since Great-Aunt Maisie and you held the handcuffs with us, we somehow went on your trip."

"And if that's the case," Maisie said, "then I know exactly where to find Great-Aunt Maisie."

Great-Uncle Thorne's eyes glistened.

"Tonight," he said. "At Tony Pastor's."

O—🔑

The crowd at Tony Pastor's was enormous. Even with three pairs of eyes searching for Great-Aunt Maisie among all the people, it was impossible to find her.

"She could be anywhere," Felix said, exhausted from being pushed and pulled.

"We can't give up now!" Great-Uncle Thorne said. "The consequences are too great."

"We've come this far," Maisie said. "We'll find her."

Maisie's eyes never left the faces around her, searching intently for that girl who stared out at them from the photograph back at Elm Medona.

An excited buzz moved through the crowd as the doors opened and people could finally take their seats.

Great-Uncle Thorne had procured seats in the front row, even though Felix had argued that it would be better to sit in the back so they could more easily look for Great-Aunt Maisie.

"Pickworths do not sit in the back," Great-Uncle Thorne had said, insulted.

Now they moved down the red-carpeted aisle toward their seats. The theater was enormous, with a high ceiling painted with Greek gods and goddesses in puffy clouds, plush, dark red seats, and a giant chandelier that glowed with hundreds of tiny bulbs.

Apparently the real star of the show was someone named Maggie Cline, a singer who sang what Great-Uncle Thorne called ridiculous tearjerkers. Great-Uncle Thorne told them her signature song, "Throw Him Down, McClosky," had a raucous, ridiculous refrain that sent everyone backstage into a frenzy whereby they threw everything and anything onto the stage, which sent the audience into a wild state.

Felix wondered if they would stay long enough to hear Maggie Cline sing "Throw Him Down, McClosky" or if they would already be back in Newport by the time she took the stage. He didn't like the next thing he thought: *Will Great-Aunt Maisie be with us when we get home?*

He didn't have time to think anything further.

Tony Pastor, a fat man with a waxed mustache and big, clunky rings on every one of his fingers, took the stage and introduced the first act. In fact, Tony Pastor introduced every act. Jugglers, dancing dogs, acrobats. Felix tried not to get distracted by what was happening on the stage and kept his eyes out for Great-Aunt Maisie.

"Ladies and gentlemen," Tony Pastor announced, "you will not believe your eyes when you watch the magic of the Prince of Air—"

At this Maisie and Felix sat at attention.

"—the European Illusionist—"

"Oh please," Great-Uncle Thorne said in disgust.

"—the remarkable, the extraordinary, the one and only Ha-arry Hou-dini!"

The red velvet curtain slowly opened.

Harry stood center stage in a yellow silk jacket and black trousers.

And there beside him, dressed in a white leotard bedazzled with sequins, stood Great-Aunt Maisie, the beautiful young assistant to Harry Houdini.

CHAPTER 12

Adieu

Maisie, Felix, and Great-Uncle Thorne sat, unable to move, as Great-Aunt Maisie assisted Harry with his act. They watched as she showed the audience the cards for his card tricks and tapped on the box to demonstrate that it was empty before he pulled an ocean of silk scarves from it. She smiled and moved gracefully across the stage, taking each of his commands. But if Great-Aunt Maisie saw them, she didn't let on.

"Ladies and gentlemen," Harry announced, "my beautiful assistant will now place not one . . . not two . . . but *three* sets of handcuffs on my wrists!"

Sixteen-year-old Great-Aunt Maisie was indeed beautiful, Felix thought as he watched her display the three sets of handcuffs to the audience, holding each one up high in front of her face and tugging hard to prove they were real. Her blue eyes were large and round and framed by long, thick lashes. She had pale skin with just the right amount of peek on her cheeks, and her blond hair bounced at her shoulders in fat curls. Felix couldn't help thinking of the Great-Aunt Maisie he knew, with a face etched with lines and creases, her eyes filmy rather than sparkling, and her hair silver.

Now she clamped each set of handcuffs on Harry's wrists, grinning wickedly as she did.

Great-Uncle Thorne turned to Felix and whispered, "Let's get out of here."

"What?" Felix whispered back. If they left, weren't they leaving Great-Aunt Maisie to a terrible fate?

"We'll wait for them outside their dressing room," Great-Uncle Thorne whispered. "Corner them."

"But we'll draw attention to ourselves if we leave right now," Felix hissed.

Onstage, Harry had just escaped from all three sets of locked handcuffs, and the audience was applauding madly.

"And now," Harry announced, articulating each

word with great care, "I will perform my most famous trick, The Metamorphosis."

Great-Uncle Thorne pressed his mouth to Felix's ear. "If they get away from us, we might get stuck here."

That was enough to get Felix up and out of his seat, pulling his sister along with him.

As Harry explained how he would lock his assistant in the trunk, Felix, Great-Uncle Thorne, and Maisie slipped up the long aisle and out into the lobby.

"In just *three* seconds, right before your eyes," Harry's voice echoed from behind them, "you will see a complete . . . metamorphosis!"

"Where are we going?" Maisie demanded.

Great-Uncle Thorne motioned for them to follow him out the door and then down the side alley that bordered the building. He stopped in front of a door that said STAGE DOOR on it.

"We've got to get Great-Aunt Maisie," Felix explained to his sister.

Maisie's head was spinning from trying to sort out what to do. Harry had those handcuffs, and all he had to do was give them some life lesson and they would go home, wouldn't they? And wouldn't Great-Aunt Maisie go with them, no matter what they did?

Great-Uncle Thorne held the stage door open for them, and Felix and Maisie found themselves in a labyrinth of corridors and rooms with closed doors. From one came the sounds of someone doing vocal warm-ups. A juggler practiced in one corridor, keeping five balls in the air while he balanced on a unicycle.

"Explain your plan," Maisie told Great-Uncle Thorne.

His eyes darted down the corridors as he tried to second-guess where his sister and Harry might emerge.

"We grab Maisie," he said, "and we take her back with us."

"But how?" Maisie demanded. "We need Harry, too, don't we?"

Great-Uncle Thorne sighed. "I'm hoping that the things he told Felix are enough to get us back. Most importantly, we need Maisie."

The sounds of the audience gasping could be heard even back here. There was a pause, and then wild applause and whistles and the stomping of feet.

"The Metamorphosis," Great-Uncle Thorne muttered as if the trick were his enemy.

To their surprise, Harry and Great-Aunt Maisie appeared, oblivious to the trap awaiting them. Hand in hand and smiling at each other, they walked toward their potential captors.

Great-Aunt Maisie saw them first.

Her blue eyes grew wide, and she stopped in her tracks.

Puzzled, Harry looked down the corridor, too.

"You again?" he said.

Maisie glanced from her great-aunt, to Harry, and then at Great-Uncle Thorne, who appeared ready to leap at his sister.

It was all too much. The hope that if they could hold on to Great-Aunt Maisie they could get home, the four of them. The consequences if they failed. Overwhelmed, Maisie turned and ran back from where they'd come, out the stage door, and onto Fourteenth Street.

She heard Felix calling for her to stop. But she didn't.

Footsteps pounded behind her. Maisie didn't bother to look over her shoulder. No doubt

Great-Uncle Thorne was after her followed by Felix. She ran faster, weaving through the crowded street. Fourteenth Street was filled with theaters, almost like Times Square was now. Theatergoers stepped outside for intermission. Carriages waited along the curb. At the corner of Fourteenth and Broadway, Maisie paused to figure out where she should go.

But a strong hand gripped her shoulder.

Maisie spun around expecting to see Great-Uncle Thorne.

Instead she found herself eye to eye with Harry Houdini.

"Why are you running?" he asked her, his voice gentle.

Maisie struggled to find a way to explain.

"It's too complicated," she said finally.

Harry's piercing eyes studied her face.

She squirmed under his grip, but he held on to her.

"Your assistant," she began.

"Also a Maisie," he said, smiling. "An angel," he added.

"She has to come back to Newport with us," Maisie said. "It's really important."

"I can't let her go. Not now that we've found each other," Harry said.

Maisie rolled her eyes at his sentimentality.

"You don't know what it's like," Harry told her. "To be different. To talk with an accent and to be poor. Without magic, I'd be . . ." He hesitated, then he said softly, "I'd be like one of the freaks."

"Ha!" Maisie said. "I *am* a freak. Not the kind who had some genetic accident, but a different kind."

She was aware of people standing closer to her, but she didn't look at them. Her eyes stayed on Harry's.

"I don't even have one friend except Felix. I invited someone over after school, and she turned out to be totally weird. Felicity LaSalle, who you call a freak—"

"Well, she is an albino," Harry said.

"She was the first person who actually wanted to be my friend." Maisie felt herself getting choked up. "So don't tell me I don't know what it's like to be different."

Harry's forehead creased with concentration.

"You need to—" he began.

"Stop!" Great-Uncle Thorne shouted, pushing through the crowd. "Don't say another word!"

Felix arrived, panting, at Maisie's side.

"Where's Great-Aunt Maisie?" Maisie asked him.

"She got away," he said.

"I believe you can find your magic," Harry said to Maisie. "Self-confidence. Discipline. Passion."

Thorne yanked Maisie away from Harry, throwing his hands over her ears.

"Look at how you improved my enunciation," Harry continued. "I believe in you. Now you just have to believe in yourself."

"Oh no!" Felix cried.

Great-Uncle Thorne's face grew wild with panic as the three of them were lifted from the sidewalk.

"Maisie!" Great-Uncle Thorne called. "Maisie!"

They heard the midway sounds of Coney Island and cannon fire and bells tinkling. The air filled with the smells of cinnamon and Christmas trees and ocean as they tumbled through it.

The last image Felix, Maisie, and Great-Uncle Thorne had was of Great-Aunt Maisie, sixteen years old and beautiful, happy and triumphant on the sidewalk across the street from where they'd stood.

She lifted her hand and waved.

They could read her lips as they traveled forward. "Adieu!" she said to them. "Adieu."

O—⚷

Maisie thought she would never forget the look on Great-Aunt Maisie's face as she called *Adieu* to them. And it was that look that she kept in her mind as she returned to the stage door in the auditorium of Anne Hutchinson Elementary School and found Great-Aunt Maisie—the real one . . . or the old one . . . or the present-day one . . . stretched out on the scuffed wooden floor and Maisie's mother yelling, "Is there a doctor in the house?"

Lily Goldberg's father came rushing up the aisle, his black doctor's bag in his hand.

"She was fine and then . . . ," their mother said.

She wrapped her arms around Maisie and Felix.

"I'm sure she'll be all right," she said in her best comforting-mother voice.

But Felix had already begun to cry.

Great-Uncle Thorne sat on one of the folding chairs, his face buried in his hands.

Lily Goldberg's father was bent over Great-Aunt Maisie, his stethoscope in his ears. The crowd had gone eerily silent, and Felix was glad that Lily came to stand beside him.

In the distance they heard the sound of a siren approaching.

The doors to the auditorium burst open, and EMTs hurried in with a stretcher, the crowd parting to let them through.

Felix couldn't bear to watch as they lifted Great-Aunt Maisie's old body onto it.

"Think of her saying adieu," Maisie told him.

And he did. He pictured her pale, unlined face, her bright blue eyes, her full lips parting to tell them good-bye.

The EMTs placed an oxygen mask over Great-Aunt Maisie's face and pulled a thin powder-blue blanket up to her chin. Lily Goldberg's father patted their mother on the back.

"There, there," he said.

Their mother looked up at him with frightened eyes.

"Will she be okay?" she asked him.

"I think it's best if you go in the ambulance with her," he said. "I can take Felix and Maisie home."

"Of course," their mother said.

She gathered Great-Aunt Maisie's wrap and purse and scurried to catch up with the EMTs.

"Do you want me to come home with you?" Lily asked Felix.

He shook his head. "We'll be okay," he said.

Great-Uncle Thorne slowly looked up, his eyes wet with tears.

"She got what she wanted," he said. "I guess we can take some comfort in that."

Maisie took Felix's hand. They had never known anyone who had died, and neither of them knew what to say or what to do.

Slowly, Great-Uncle Thorne got to his feet. He put his arms around their shoulders, leaning on them a bit for support, his walking stick dangling from his hand. The three of them made their way across the auditorium and out into the spring night. The air had gone still, and the sky seemed to have filled with more stars than they ever had seen. They stood on the sidewalk, waiting for Dr. Goldberg to get his car and take them back to Elm Medona.

A breeze cut through the still night air, growing in intensity, shaking the new leaves on the trees.

Maisie and Felix inhaled. They could smell things

blossoming, coming to life. Ever so faintly they caught a whiff of Chanel No. 5.

Adieu!

The breeze seemed to carry that word with it.

Adieu!

Great-Uncle Thorne, Maisie, and Felix each lifted their faces upward as if they could catch it.

Adieu!

Then the breeze was gone, and everything went still and silent again.

HARRY HOUDINI
March 24, 1874–October 31, 1926

For most of his life, Harry Houdini said that he was born in Appleton, Wisconsin. However, he was really born Ehrich Weisz in Budapest, Hungary. His father, a rabbi, immigrated to the United States when Harry was four. There, he changed the family's last name from Weisz to Weiss. The congregation in Appleton found Harry's father to be too old-fashioned, and he was fired. When Harry was eight, the family moved to Milwaukee. They were quite poor, and all the children had to work when they were young. Harry sold newspapers and worked shining shoes.

Harry's father took him to see a magician who called himself Dr. Lynn. Soon afterward, Harry began performing magic tricks in the backyard. Although he claimed to have performed a trapeze act in which he hung upside down and picked up pins with his eyelids, this is widely thought to be an exaggeration of a simple trick he did hanging from a tree in his family's backyard wearing red socks his mother made for him. Still, he did call himself "Ehrich, Prince of the Air."

At the age of twelve, Harry ran away from home by hopping on a freight train to Kansas City. He stayed away for a year, during which his family moved to New York City in the hopes of finding work. Harry joined them there, taking jobs as a tie cutter, messenger, and photographer's assistant to help the family survive. He became a prizewinning cross-country runner and swimmer, beginning the discipline of exercise that continued throughout his life.

A friend gave Harry the book *The Memoirs of Robert-Houdin: Ambassador, Author, and Conjuror, Written by Himself* about the famous French magician who had lived in the mid-1800s and was considered the father of modern magic. The book changed Harry's life. A friend told him, erroneously, that in French, adding an *i* to *Houdin* would mean "like Houdin," the great magician. So Harry added an *i* to his idol's name. He also thought it sounded more mysterious. The name Harry came from a mispronunciation or an Americanization of his Hungarian nickname, Ehrie. At any rate, Harry Houdini was born.

After his father died, seventeen-year-old Harry and his brother Theo, called Dash, became The Brothers Houdini, performing their magic act at dime museums, civic groups, sideshows, and music halls around the city, including the famous amusement park Coney Island. There he met a young singer named Bess Rahner. They fell in love, and soon Bess replaced Dash, becoming Harry's assistant. Bess and Harry got married and traveled with circuses performing his magic act, which included The Metamorphosis.

But Harry wanted to become famous. He began to perfect becoming an escape artist. An expert at escaping from handcuffs, Houdini would arrive in a new town and claim the ability to escape from any handcuffs provided by the local police, offering $100 to anyone who provided handcuffs from which he could not escape. He never had to pay. Soon he was known as "The Handcuff King."

In London, he successfully broke free after being wrapped around a pillar and handcuffed at Scotland Yard. Word of this escape spread throughout Europe, and soon his act was sold out everywhere he went. Harry performed a stunt in which he was handcuffed and chained while nailed into a packing crate that was then thrown into a river. Realizing that the crowd loved the suspense and the danger, he would remain underwater long after many observers were certain he couldn't survive. Then he would pop up, waving the chains over his head.

The Houdinis returned to the United States in

1905 as international celebrities. Harry's stunts became more sensational and more difficult. Houdini escaped from the prison cell that held the assassin of President James Garfield and freed himself from a straitjacket while hanging upside down. He regularly was shackled and lowered into an oversize milk can filled with water and then hidden by a curtain. Though he could escape in three minutes, Houdini frequently made the audience wait as long as half an hour before reappearing. The possibility of failure and death thrilled his audiences. Eventually, Houdini invited the public to devise contraptions to hold him. These included everything from boilers to mailbags to the belly of a whale that had washed ashore in Boston.

In 1912, Houdini introduced what is considered his most famous act, the Chinese Water Torture Cell. He was suspended upside down in a locked glass-and-steel cabinet full to overflowing with water. The act required that Houdini hold his breath for more than three minutes. By the fall of 1926, Houdini's show included not only the Chinese Water Torture Cell trick, but also escapes from a coffin, straitjacket, and challenges from the audience. The performance took two and a half hours and required him to be onstage almost the entire time.

The tour took a bad turn in Providence, Rhode Island, when Bess contracted a case of food poisoning. Despite the presence of a nurse, Houdini was deeply worried about his wife and stayed awake all night at her side. Exhausted, he insisted on performing, anyway, in Albany, New York. That night, the frame holding his leg in place for the Chinese water torture jerked, and his ankle broke. Against the advice of a doctor, Houdini continued on to his next performance in Montreal.

In his dressing room, a fan who was also an amateur boxer asked if it was true that Houdini could withstand any blow to his body above the waist, excluding his face. Houdini gave the student permission to test him. He began to get up, but before he had time to tighten his abdomen muscles, the student punched him three times in the stomach. Despite excruciating pain, Houdini performed his show that afternoon. The next day, with the chills and sweating of a high fever, Houdini performed two more shows and then continued on to Detroit, Michigan. There, with a temperature of 102, a doctor ordered him to go immediately to the hospital. Instead, Houdini performed that night.

After the show, he finally went to the hospital. But by this time, his appendix had burst and he had peritonitis, an infection caused by the rupture that was often fatal before the development of antibiotics. Knowing he was dying, Houdini told Bess that he would communicate with her from beyond the grave. She would know it was really him if she heard the words "Rosabelle, believe." "Rosabelle" was the name of a song that Bess had sung at Coney Island when she met Houdini.

Harry Houdini died on Halloween. Every Halloween for as long as she lived, Bess held a séance, trying to communicate with Harry. But she died in 1943 without ever succeeding.

I do so much research for each book in The Treasure Chest series and discover so many cool facts that I can't fit into every book. Here are some of my favorites from my research for *The Treasure Chest: #4 Harry Houdini: Prince of Air*. Enjoy!

Coney Island at the end of the nineteenth century and beginning of the twentieth century was the most popular amusement park in the country. But originally, amusement parks were located in medieval Europe and were called "pleasure gardens." However, these did not have rides. Instead, they had live entertainment, dancing, games, and restaurants. Pleasure gardens offered people the opportunity to escape the city. The oldest one still standing is Bakken, which is north of Copenhagen, Denmark, and opened in 1583.

The first amusement park in the United States opened on July 4, 1894 in Chicago. Until then, the amusement parks' attractions were beautiful beaches and picnic grounds or restaurants. They were usually located at the end of a trolley line so that visitors could reach them easily. But a swimmer and showman named Paul Boyton changed that when he opened Paul Boyton's Water Chute, which focused not on natural attractions but on mechanical ones. It was so successful that the next year he opened another one in Coney Island, New York.

Boyton's idea was influenced by the 1893 Chicago World's Fair or the World's Columbian Exposition. World fairs began in London about forty years earlier as a way to celebrate industrial achievement. Soon, American cities began hosting world fairs, too. The Chicago World's Fair was held in an enclosed site, and strived to merge entertainment, education, and engineering. Its midway was lined with ornate buildings, and lit with many streetlamps, which not only allowed people to go there at night but also served to dazzle them with their brightness. One area, the Midway Plaisance, was dedicated to amusements. The first Ferris wheel was there. All of these elements became the mainstay of amusement parks. By 1910, there were more than two thousand amusement parks in the United States.

The Gilded Age, the era in which Phinneas Pickworth and the other wealthy denizens of Newport built their mansions, was a time when many people had disposable income and much leisure time. They wanted new forms of entertainment, and amusement parks matched their desires. By the 1920s, this era was sometimes called the "golden age of roller coasters" because people wanted faster and faster roller coasters, with higher hills and longer drops.

The three rides that you could find at any amusement park were the Ferris wheel, roller coaster, and carousel. Here is how they came to be:

THE FERRIS WHEEL:

The Ferris wheel was invented by George W. Ferris for the 1893 Chicago World's Fair. Ferris was a bridge builder in Pittsburgh. At a dinner with the organizers of the fair, Ferris learned that they wanted something to rival the Eiffel Tower in Paris. The Eiffel Tower, designed by Gustav Eiffel, was built for the Exposition Universelle—or the Paris World's Fair—in 1889, which also celebrated the hundredth anniversary of the French Revolution. During the dinner, Ferris drew his design on a napkin.

Rival the Eiffel Tower it did! Considered an engineering marvel, the first Ferris wheel had two

140-foot steel towers that supported it. The forty-five-foot axle that connected them was the largest single piece of forged steel ever made. The wheel's diameter was 250 feet; its circumference was 825 feet. It took two 1,000-horsepower reversible engines to make the ride work. And there were thirty-six wooden cars, which held up to sixty riders each. It cost fifty cents to ride the Ferris wheel. That ride consisted of one revolution with nine stops to reload the cars, and one nonstop revolution.

THE ROLLER COASTER:

The first roller coasters were ice slides in Russia, which were built during the 1600s. Wood structures were covered with ice, and riders slid down them on wooden sleds or sleds made of ice. Sometime in the mid-1780s, they introduced wheeled vehicles, and by 1817, these "cars" were locked to the tracks. When we think of roller coasters today, we always picture them with a loop. The first roller coaster to have a loop was in Paris in 1846; the loop was thirteen feet wide. The first roller coaster built in the United States was the Switchback Railway at Coney Island in 1884.

These early roller coasters were made out of wood.

And during the 1920s—the "golden age of roller coasters"—some of the most famous wooden roller coasters were built: Santa Cruz Beach Boardwalk's Giant Dipper, Coney Island's Cyclone, the Big Dipper at Geauga Lake in Bainbridge Township, Ohio, and The Thriller at Euclid Beach Park in Cleveland. Only The Thriller is no longer operating. And I am happy to report that I have ridden both the Cyclone and the Giant Dipper!

THE CAROUSEL:

Carousels are also known as "painted ponies" and merry-go-rounds. The word *carousel* comes from an Italian word—*carosello*, which means "little war." Anyone who has ridden a carousel can probably understand why they are sometimes called painted ponies: the carousels popular at amusement parks, especially from the late 1800s until about 1930, had elaborately carved and painted horses to ride. And the word *merry-go-round* captures the happy rotations of riding a carousel. But "little war"?

In the twelfth century, *carosello* was a popular game played on horseback by Arabs and Turks. Players threw scented balls back and forth, which broke when they hit someone, so the losers could be identified by how they smelled! Later, in France, *carosello* became *carousel* and was used to describe equestrian pageants. One of the competitions in a carousel involved catching a ring that had been hung from a post while riding a horse at full speed. In order to practice for this competition, knights sat on wooden horses on a rotating platform with a ring at its center. Soon, women and children began riding the practice machine for fun.

Even today, some carousels have brass rings that riders try to catch as they pass, including the Flying Horse Carousel in Oak Bluffs, Massachusetts, the Crescent Park Carousel in Riverside, Rhode Island, and the Flying Horse Carousel in Westerly, Rhode Island, all of which were built in the 1890s.

DISNEYLAND:

The Great Depression in the 1930s led to the demise of amusement parks in the United States. It began when the stock market crashed in October of 1929 and didn't end until World War II. During that time, millions of Americans were unemployed. In fact, in 1932 in New York City alone one million people did not have jobs. Gone were the days of spending time—and money—in amusement parks. Maintaining and creating the rides became impossible and many amusement parks went into decline. Instead of being the glittering, innovative places they once were, amusement parks became associated with grit and grime.

Until Walt Disney decided to create a whole new version of the amusement park.

Walt Disney was born in 1901, and became a cartoonist at a commercial art studio in Kansas City. In 1923, his brother Roy, who lived in Los Angeles, urged Walt to move there and make animated films. Twenty years later, Walt Disney Studio had created Mickey Mouse, Pluto, Goofy, and Donald Duck, among other now-famous cartoon characters.

When Walt Disney conceived his idea for a new kind of amusement park, he wanted it to be different from the deteriorated ones that existed in the mid-twentieth century. Instead, he envisioned a place with no roller coasters, no hot-dog stands, no alcohol sold—a place where a family could wander down a replica of Main Street, U.S.A., and meet the cartoon characters he had created. Main Street would lead to many different Disney theme parks, where families could escape the hardships and realities of daily life.

But no one else could see Walt Disney's dream the way he did. His brother Roy refused to invest in the plan, and he couldn't find other financial backers. He had to find cheap land near a major highway, just as early amusement parks had to be built at the end of trolley lines. Eventually, Disney bought 160 acres of orange grove in Anaheim, California. In 1954, construction of Disneyland began.

Opening day, July 17, 1955, was a disaster in many ways. Temperatures were over one hundred degrees, and due to a plumbers' strike, none of the water fountains worked. Visitors thought Disney had purposely turned off the water to force them to pay for drinks. That day, so many people came to Disneyland that the park was overcrowded and workers there quickly grew short tempered. Popular rides had long lines while unpopular ones were empty. Admission to rides was made even slower because each ride required its own ticket, making ticket lines long as well. That first week, with temperatures staying over one hundred degrees, crowds decreased. Fantasyland sprang a gas leak. When the popular television character Davy Crockett (played by Fess Parker) made his grand appearance, water sprinklers came on and soaked him. An overcrowded boat almost capsized. The press began calling Walt Disney's dream a nightmare.

But rather than getting discouraged, Disney set out to solve all of the opening-week problems. He invented an admission system that allowed entry to all the attractions. He redesigned all of the water fountains, trash cans, and restrooms so that even they reflected the themes of the park. He also trained all park employees in park etiquette. After a shaky start, Disneyland had one million visitors within six months. A decade later, it had had fifty million visitors.

In 1959, Walt Disney set his sights on a second park. When he flew over swampland outside Orlando, Florida, and saw the network of developed roads there, he began to buy up the land. Although Disney died in 1966, his vision for Disney World became a reality when it opened in 1971. Today, it is the most visited theme park in the world.

Continue your adventures in
The Treasure Chest!

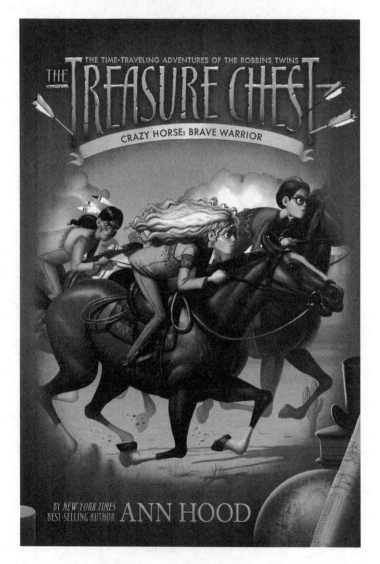